The second kiss was even more passionate than the first. Jessica felt herself being transported. *As long as this kiss lasts, Christian and I really* are *the only two people in the world,* she thought.

She was swept away by the delirious pleasure of the moment, but not so completely that she didn't notice a movement out of the corner of her eye. Someone had entered the foyer of the restaurant. *The host, or a waiter,* Jessica thought distractedly, too happy to be embarrassed. *Oh, well. Nothing this good could last forever.*

With a delicious, regretful sigh, she opened her eyes a little wider, looking past Christian's shoulder. Then she focused on the figure standing in the doorway, and her heart stopped beating.

A rangy, broad-shouldered blond guy in khakis and a blue polo shirt stood just inside the entrance to the cafe, an expression of mingled shock, hurt, and anger contorting his handsome face.

Jessica's heart started up again, but now it was hammering with guilt and horror. She tore herself from Christian's embrace.

"Ken!" she cried.

THE HIGH SCHOOL WAR

Written by
Kate William

Created by
FRANCINE PASCAL

BANTAM BOOKS
NEW YORK • TORONTO • LONDON • SYDNEY • AUCKLAND

To Jonathan David Rubin

RL 6, age 12 and up

THE HIGH SCHOOL WAR
A Bantam Book / February 1996

Sweet Valley High® is a registered trademark of Francine Pascal
Conceived by Francine Pascal
Produced by Daniel Weiss Associates, Inc.
33 West 17th Street
New York, NY 10011
Cover art by Bruce Emmett

ISBN: 0-553-56639-3

Published simultaneously in the United States and Canada

Bantam Books are published by Bantam Books, a division of Bantam Doubleday Dell Publishing Group, Inc. Its trademark, consisting of the words "Bantam Books" and the portrayal of a rooster, is Registered in U.S. Patent and Trademark Office and in other countries. Marca Registrada. Bantam Books, 1540 Broadway, New York, New York 10036.

PRINTED IN THE UNITED STATES OF AMERICA

OPM 0 9 8 7 6 5 4 3 2 1

Chapter 1

Sixteen-year-old Jessica Wakefield's eyelids fluttered. *I must have fainted,* she thought, feeling dizzy and confused. She struggled to sit up, her fingernails scraping cold, hard gravel. *Where am I?* she wondered groggily. *What happened?*

She was dimly aware of the chaos whirling around her. People raced past in the night, their footsteps pounding on the pavement. There were urgent shouts, and sirens wailed in the distance, growing closer. *That's right,* Jessica remembered. *I'm in the vacant lot next to the warehouse. The dance. The fight!*

Gradually, her blue-green eyes came into focus. A dark-haired boy in a ripped Palisades High School T-shirt knelt next to her. Jessica stared into his face as if seeing it for the first time, even though every feature was intimately familiar to her. "Christian," she whispered.

"Hey, Gorman, let's get out of here!" someone yelled. "The cops are coming—we'll all get busted."

Christian Gorman shot a glance over his shoulder. As the police cars drew closer, the boys who'd been involved in the Sweet Valley High–Palisades High brawl scattered. Jessica glimpsed her boyfriend, Ken Matthews, being dragged off by Bruce Patman. Only Christian hung back.

He turned once again to Jessica, his handsome face pale. Blood dripped from a cut on his cheekbone. "Meet me at the beach tomorrow morning," he said hoarsely.

Jessica knew she should say no. With her own eyes she'd just seen Christian punch out Ken. To her utter dismay she'd discovered that the mysterious boy she'd met on the beach one magical dawn—the boy who was teaching her to surf, the boy she'd fallen madly, secretly in love with—was from Palisades. Not only that, but he was actually the *leader* of the gang that was feuding with her own Sweet Valley classmates and friends. *He's the enemy,* she reminded herself. *I should hate him. I should tell him I never want to see him again.*

Instead, still staring into Christian's smoky blue eyes, she nodded weakly. "Tomorrow," she agreed. "Now, go. You have to get out of here!"

Christian hesitated a moment longer, his hand strong and supportive on Jessica's arm. Then, as the flashing lights of a squad car neared the parking lot, he leaped to his feet and sprinted off, melting into the darkness.

Elizabeth Wakefield fought her way through the crowded party. The Droids, a popular Sweet Valley High rock band, were cranking out one of their liveliest tunes. But even with the music blasting, the renovated warehouse the two high schools had rented for the masked costume ball still seemed gloomy and unwelcoming. Elizabeth sighed when she remembered all the work that had gone into the streamers and balloons draped festively from the rafters. Nobody was dancing and no one mingled. Instead, students clustered together in strictly segregated groups: Sweet Valley on one side, Palisades on the other.

Elizabeth caught snatches of conversation—rumors flew faster than the wind gusting through the open door at the rear of the warehouse. "A huge fight," one student exclaimed.

"Palisades High started it," said her companion.

"And Sweet Valley's outnumbered!" another person contributed.

Elizabeth's best friend, Enid Rollins, hurried with her to the exit. "I'm glad we called the police," Elizabeth told Enid, relieved to hear the sound of approaching sirens. "I knew there'd be trouble when the guys went outside. Bruce and Todd and the rest of the gang have been out for blood ever since the Palisades bunch nailed their houses with toilet paper and eggs."

"I just hope no one's hurt," Enid fretted.

"Me, too," Elizabeth said.

The rivalry had started heating up a few weeks ago. During the Sweet Valley High–Palisades High football game, the Palisades team had played dirty, injuring a few of Sweet Valley's best players. After the game the victorious Palisades linebacker, Greg McMullen, had insulted Sweet Valley's quarterback, Ken Matthews, and then punched him in the stomach. If their friends hadn't restrained them, Ken and Greg would have wound up fighting.

The Sweet Valley boys had got revenge for Palisades's dirty-game tactics by spray-painting "Palisades Pumas Purr Like Kittens" on the Palisades High School football field. A few days later the Palisades boys raided Sweet Valley after dark, nailing selected houses and cars with toilet paper and eggs.

"I guess this dance was a bad idea," Enid said to Elizabeth. "We were crazy to bring the two schools together."

"Maybe it's not so bad out there," said Elizabeth, clinging to a faint thread of hope. "Todd has *some* sense. He won't let the guys do anything stupid. Maybe they're just talking things over."

She and Enid managed to push their way through the crush and out the door into the parking lot behind the warehouse. Not seeing anyone, they ran around the side of the building. "It *is* a fight!" Enid shrieked.

Sure enough, at the far end of the gravel-and-weed-filled vacant lot, a few shadowy figures grappled while others sprinted away. Elizabeth's heart thumped fearfully. Was that Todd, disappearing into the night? Ken? Bruce, Winston? In the darkness she couldn't be sure.

A few seconds later the boys had all taken off, leaving only one person behind. A body lay prone on the gravel. "Someone's injured," Enid exclaimed. "And it looks like—"

"A girl," said Elizabeth. A girl in a black halter dress, with long golden blond hair just like Elizabeth's. "Jessica!" Elizabeth cried.

Elizabeth rushed to her twin's side. "Jess, are you all right?" she squeaked, her voice shrill with terror. As she cradled Jessica in her arms, Elizabeth saw that her sister's dress was splattered with drops of something shiny—blood. "What did they do to you?"

"I'm OK," Jessica assured Elizabeth, sitting up and brushing the grit from her hands. "I just passed out or something when I saw—when I saw—" Jessica glanced down at her dress and shuddered. "That's not my blood. Someone must have dripped on me."

Elizabeth and Enid helped Jessica to her feet. As a police car swerved into the lot, lights flashing and tires screeching, two girls joined the Sweet Valley trio: Marla Daniels and Caitlin Alexander from Palisades High School, the new friends who'd helped Elizabeth organize the dance.

"The guys took off, huh?" said Marla.

Caitlin stared at the blood on Jessica's dress with wide brown eyes. "It must've been a bad fight, though," she murmured.

"I hope Doug's all right!"

"At least it's over," said Enid.

"Unless they ran off to finish their business somewhere else," Marla replied ominously.

Jessica buried her face in her hands. "Liz, it was awful. When I saw Ken and—" Her voice broke on a sob.

Elizabeth put an arm around her twin's shoulders, her own cheeks damp with tears. Just as Caitlin was worried about her boyfriend, Doug Riker, Elizabeth couldn't help wondering what had happened to Todd. Was he OK, or was that *his* blood staining Jessica's dress? "We'll never be able to make peace now," Elizabeth choked out, stroking

Jessica's tangled hair. "Look what happened when we tried to get the two schools together! And it's all my fault."

"It's not your fault," Enid declared. "You're not responsible, Liz. You didn't start this feud."

"You're definitely not to blame," Marla confirmed, "but I'm afraid we're not dealing with a feud anymore. It's beyond that now. Way beyond."

As a uniformed police officer strode toward them, Elizabeth had to agree. The peace of their idyllic southern California community had been shattered. That night the bad blood between Sweet Valley and Palisades had erupted like a long-dormant volcano. "This isn't normal high school rivalry," Elizabeth said. "It's a high school *war*."

Sweet Valley High's star quarterback, Ken Matthews, ran swiftly through the dark alley, his arms pumping as though he were sprinting down the football field to make a touchdown. Tall, long-legged Todd Wilkins kept pace at Ken's side. Ahead of them, Bruce Patman hurdled a fallen trash can, then dodged left down a deserted street. "Where on earth are we going, Patman?" Todd called.

Bruce slowed slightly so Todd, Ken, and the other Sweet Valley High boys who'd fought with Palisades could catch up to him. "I staked out the area this afternoon," Bruce panted. "There's an abandoned warehouse another quarter mile down the road with some windows broken on the ground floor. C'mon, we're almost there."

A few minutes later the boys collapsed inside the warehouse, huffing and puffing. Bruce took a flashlight from his pocket and scanned their faces. Aaron Dallas had a black eye. Football player Zack Johnson's nose was bleeding. Todd's jaw was bruised and swollen, while Ronnie Edwards's cheek was scraped raw. Ken himself could feel blood dripping down his chin from a split lip.

Only one of the Sweet Valley boys appeared to have escaped unhurt. "How'd you manage to stay so clean and pretty?" Bruce asked Winston Egbert sarcastically.

Class clown Winston Egbert flashed his trademark grin, though his eyes were somber. "I'm a lover, not a fighter," he kidded. "Seriously, though. I was in there with you guys, but I was trying to break things up." He pointed to Bruce's bloody nose. "Guess you were too busy getting pounded by that bum from Palisades to hear me yelling at you to cool it."

"For your information, I didn't get pounded," Bruce snapped. "I gave as good as I got. Another thirty seconds and that guy would've been history."

Ken punched the floor, cursing under his breath. "When you were dragging me off," he muttered to Todd, "I saw that Palisades guy, the one who jumped me. I'm pretty sure he went over to Jessica and said something to her. You should've let me stay with her, man."

"You heard the sirens," Todd reasoned. He massaged his ankle, which had been in a walking cast until just a week ago, after he'd broken it during a basketball game. "We were about to get into major trouble. Would you rather be in jail right now?"

Ken scowled. "But she fainted or something. She didn't look too good." He lifted a hand to his face, gingerly touching his split lip, and his blood boiled with frustration. He punched the floor again. "I hate not getting a chance to finish what I started. All I can say is, if that guy said something crude to Jessica, he's going to hear from me."

Todd rested a hand on Ken's shoulder. "Take it easy, Matthews. I'm sure Jess is OK."

Ken tried to tune back in to Bruce, who'd been ranting and raving ever since they'd reached the hideout. One word in particular seized Ken's attention. ". . . revenge," Bruce was saying. "They roughed us up tonight because they outnumbered us, and they caught us off guard—we weren't going to stoop so low as to start anything at a stupid school dance. Then the cops came before we could get back on our feet and really fight back. But next time . . ."

"Next time?" Winston raked a hand through his rumpled brown hair. "Do we really want a rematch?"

"You bet," declared Bruce. "I want to get my hands on the jerk who gave me this bloody nose."

"I don't know." Todd rubbed his bruised jaw. "Maybe we should let the whole thing drop. We hate Palisades, they hate us—leave it at that. What's the point of beating each other to a pulp?"

"Todd's right," Winston agreed. "Besides, if they did this much damage to us during a fight the police broke up before it even really got started, we'd get *killed* in an all-out rumble."

Todd held up his hands. "Whoa. I didn't say we should back down."

Winston's comment hit a nerve with Ken, too. "Yeah, are you saying you don't think we could beat them?" he demanded, sitting up straight.

Winston shrugged. "No, but in my humble opinion, we'd be better off—"

"We'll be better off when we waste those guys, once and for all," Bruce interrupted.

Todd's eyes flashed sparks. "They won't stand a chance against us in a fair fight."

All around the room, the declaration was echoed. Instead of cooling the fire, Winston had stoked it hotter. "They'll be sorry they ever set foot in Sweet Valley," Ronnie predicted fiercely.

"But they're not going to be safe even if they

stay in Palisades," Bruce growled. "I say it's time to carry the battle back to their home turf."

Aaron jumped to his feet. "Justice," he shouted. "That's all we're after!"

Adrenaline coursed through Ken's veins. He remembered the jolt of pain as the Palisades guy's fist crashed into his face. He pictured Jessica, limp and helpless, forced to listen to crude insults. *And I still owe them for what they did to my players during the football game,* Ken thought. *Bryce's concussion and Rick's messed-up knee.* He agreed with Bruce completely. They couldn't just sit around and talk about revenge. It was their duty to take action. Their pride, and the pride of Sweet Valley, was at stake.

"Justice," Ken repeated, his voice ringing strong and clear in the cavernous warehouse.

There were now three police cars pulled up next to the warehouse where the dance was being held. The parking lot was packed with students who'd flooded outside, drawn by the shouts and the sirens. An officer lifted a bullhorn to his mouth. "The party's over, kids," he bellowed. "Get in your cars and go on home."

There were grumbles of protest, but almost immediately the crowd began to disperse. *I've got to get out of here,* Jessica thought. But she couldn't seem to lift her feet to walk away from the scene of the fight. Still reeling from what she'd just learned, she felt as if she might faint again at any moment.

Christian Gorman went to Palisades High School. He was one of them!

Was there any way she could have known that? It had all started so innocently. One day at Ocean Bay, watching the Rock-TV host interviewing some surfers, she and Lila had made a playful bet. Jessica had determined to learn to surf so she could enter a Rock-TV-sponsored contest. Lila, meanwhile, had promised to wear hot pink zinc oxide on her nose for a week if Jessica won the grand prize, an all-expenses-paid trip to Hawaii. If Jessica lost, she'd have to wear a wet suit to school.

I waxed Steven's old surfboard, Jessica recalled, *and dragged myself out there at dawn that first morning. I had no idea what I was doing and the very first wave wiped me out.* She'd thought the board was gone for good, but then Christian had sauntered up with it and asked, "Were you looking for this?"

He was drop-dead gorgeous, with ocean blue eyes, wavy dark hair, and a deeply tanned, muscular body. The attraction had been instantaneous, and mutual. When he'd offered to give her surfing lessons, it hadn't even occurred to her to refuse. They'd started meeting at the beach every morning before school, and soon they weren't just talking about how to ride a wave. They were talking about love. It had been like an unbelievably sexy, romantic fantasy—only it was real. When she'd least expected it, the boy of her dreams had walked, living and breathing, into her life.

The first time he kissed me, I knew it was wrong, Jessica remembered with a pang. She'd felt terrible cheating on Ken, especially after what had happened when she and Elizabeth had recently visited their older brother, Steven, at Sweet Valley University. While she'd been away, Jessica had gotten involved with a boy named Zack Marsden. Ken had been pretty hurt about her dating someone else, and she'd sworn it would never happen again. But her feelings for Christian were irresistible.

Still, even though she knew she was playing with fire, Jessica had been lulled into a feeling of security. She and Christian had agreed to tell each other very few personal details—she knew next to nothing about where he lived, what school he went to, what his family was like. They existed for each other only in the magic of those mornings as they paddled their boards out into the surf, then later basked on the sand in each other's arms.

Their romance had been secret, apart from the real world. Now Jessica's eyes burned with unshed tears. If only it could have stayed that way. If only the magic, the illusion, could have lasted forever.

A voice broke into her reverie. "I didn't see anything, Officer," Elizabeth was saying, "but I think my sister might have."

Jessica blinked. The Sweet Valley policeman was turning toward her. *Oh, no,* thought Jessica, taking a giant step backward. *Why did I stick around? I can't talk to the police!*

She whirled, preparing to scurry after the rest of the departing students, and ran smack into another police officer. The woman grasped Jessica's arm in a gentle but firm grip. "If you don't mind coming to the station with us, miss, we'd like to take a statement from you," the policewoman said. "You appear to be the only eyewitness."

Jessica groaned silently, but there was no point protesting—she was cornered. Within seconds she found herself swiftly ushered into one of the squad cars with Elizabeth. The officer gunned the engine, and, lights flashing, they sped toward police headquarters in downtown Sweet Valley.

In the backseat Jessica slumped, staring out the window with despondent eyes. "You appear to be the only eyewitness. . . . We'd like to take a statement . . ."

Remembered images of the fight between Palisades and Sweet Valley High flickered through her brain, a mad ballet of swinging arms, bodies leaping and falling. She saw Christian, her new love, transformed into a frightening stranger as his fist smashed into Ken Matthews's face.

Jessica hugged herself, clenching her jaw to keep her teeth from chattering. They could ask her all the questions they liked, but she wouldn't tell them what she'd seen. She couldn't.

Chapter 2

Elizabeth gave Jessica's hand a reassuring squeeze. "Don't look so scared, Jess," she said lightly. "You're not under arrest! They just want some information."

They were seated across from Officer Donna Claiborne's desk at the Sweet Valley police station. Now that some time had passed, Elizabeth expected her twin to have regained her composure. But Jessica didn't smile. She sat with her arms folded tightly across her chest and her shoulders hunched, her chin down and eyes averted so that her long blond hair fell in a curtain before her face. *She's still shaking,* Elizabeth observed with surprise.

Elizabeth was puzzled. It really wasn't like Jessica to get so upset about something like this. The twins were identical in appearance only—

when it came to personality, their father liked to say the twins were like avocados and oranges. Elizabeth focused her energy on projects, goals, relationships. She threw herself into her schoolwork and her column for the Sweet Valley High newspaper and never lost sight of her dream of becoming a professional writer. Still, she always had time for her friends, and especially her boyfriend, Todd. In contrast, Jessica's energy and interests were scattered like a handful of sand tossed into the wind. She was the daredevil sister—she'd try anything if it promised to be fun and possibly a little bit dangerous. Life was too short to play by the rules: That was Jessica's chief motto.

The more Elizabeth thought about it, the more Jessica's fainting seemed distinctly out of character. *I would've thought she'd get a kick out of the fight, be egging Ken and the guys on,* Elizabeth mused. *Doing her cheerleader thing.*

Officer Claiborne looked at Jessica, her pen poised. The other policeman who'd accompanied them to the station, Officer Ken McCue, joined them. "I know it's late, so we won't keep you long," Officer Claiborne promised. "We just need to fill out a report on the disturbance at the dance. Can you tell us how it started?"

Jessica kept her eyes down and remained silent. "Actually, I was the one who dialed nine-one-one,"

Elizabeth said. "I was on the planning committee for the dance—we were hoping it would create some good feelings between the two schools. You know, socializing, getting to know each other. There'd been some scuffles, a few pranks. Nothing serious," she hastened to add, not wanting to get Todd and the other boys into more trouble than they were already in. "But pretty much as soon as the party started, the Palisades High guys said something to the Sweet Valley guys, a challenge or something. The next thing we knew, the guys had all gone outside. Some of the girls were worried there might be a fight, so we called the police."

"But you didn't actually see the fight," observed Officer Claiborne, scribbling in her notebook.

Elizabeth shook her head. "That's where Jessica comes in."

They all waited for Jessica to speak, but she kept her lips tightly pressed together. After a minute Officer Claiborne prodded her. "Ms. Wakefield, when you entered the vacant lot next to the warehouse, was the fight still in progress?"

Jessica hesitated a fraction of a second. "N-no," she murmured, avoiding the policewoman's penetrating gaze. "I think there were some people at the far end, but I really didn't see anything."

"But you fainted."

Jessica shrugged. "I just fell. I must've tripped."

"The blood on your dress." Officer Claiborne checked her notebook. "Your sister said that you said it wasn't your blood—someone else dripped blood on you. It must have been one of the boys who was fighting. Can you tell us the names of any of the Sweet Valley students? Did you recognize any of the Palisades High boys?"

Elizabeth held her breath. *Here it comes,* she thought. *She'll say she saw Todd and Ken and Bruce. Then the guys will probably be arrested!*

Jessica shot a fast glance at Elizabeth. "No," she muttered. "Like I said, I didn't see any of them close-up."

"Are you sure?" pressed Officer Claiborne. "You didn't recognize any of your schoolmates?"

"I didn't see anything," Jessica repeated stubbornly.

Elizabeth stared at her sister, puzzled. *She didn't recognize anyone, not a single person? That's not what she said before.* Then all at once she thought she understood why Jessica was changing her story. She was protecting Ken.

Elizabeth couldn't believe Jessica would lie outright to the police, but at the same time, she was immensely relieved. Todd and Ken and the other guys wouldn't get into trouble. If Jessica didn't reveal their names, there was nothing the police could do.

After a few more minutes of futile questioning,

Officer Claiborne threw up her hands. "This isn't going anywhere."

"It looks like we'll have to chalk this up to a long-standing high-school rivalry and hope it doesn't happen again," Officer McCue confirmed.

"Can we go now?" Jessica asked, rising from her seat.

Officer Claiborne sighed, then nodded. "Come on. I'll drive you home."

The twins followed the policewoman outside. After they climbed in back of the squad car, Elizabeth jiggled her sister's arm and tried to catch her eye, but Jessica just slouched in her seat, her face turned toward the window. From the side, Elizabeth could see that Jessica's cheek was damp with tears. "Jess, what's the matter?" she whispered. "You *did* see something, and it's really bothering you. Was it because Ken was there? Do you want to talk about it?"

Jessica shook her head, but the tears were flowing faster.

"It's OK," Elizabeth murmured, patting her sister's knee. "I'm sure Ken and Todd are OK. At least I hope they are," she added, her forehead wrinkling with concern. As the squad car raced through the darkness, bearing her and Jessica home to the Wakefield house on Calico Drive, Elizabeth realized that the night wasn't over yet. She wouldn't be able to fall asleep until she heard from Todd, until she found out what had really happened after the boys from the two rival high schools had left the dance . . . and she found out what Jessica had seen that had made her faint.

"Ken! What are you doing here?" squeaked Jessica.

Ned and Alice Wakefield had been shocked, to put it mildly, when their sixteen-year-old daughters arrived home from the dance in a police car. After telling their parents about the trip to the police station and the reason for it, Elizabeth had gone to bed. Not feeling the least bit sleepy, Jessica had rummaged in the fridge for a snack. Now she was sitting outside in the moonlight with the family's golden retriever, Prince Albert.

She hadn't noticed Ken crossing the shadowy lawn. She put a hand to her fast-beating heart. "You scared me half to death!"

"Sorry," Ken said. "I just couldn't head home without first coming by to make sure you were all right." When he brushed a strand of hair off her forehead, she shivered. "*Are* you all right? You still seem jittery."

Jessica stepped away from him, pretending to reach for Prince Albert's collar. "Yeah, I'm fine."

"I'm sorry you walked right into the middle of that scene." Ken's blue eyes were warm with concern. "And I'm sorry I ran away like that. But

Wilkins hauled me off—the cops were coming, and it wasn't going to look too good."

Did he notice? she wondered, her heart still pounding like a jackhammer. *Did he see me and Christian?* "Don't worry about it," she said.

"I couldn't help worrying." Ken clenched his fists. "When I saw that guy . . ."

Jessica gulped. "W-what guy?"

"Some jerk from Palisades." Ken lifted a hand to his bruised face. "The one who belted me. Did he say something to you?"

"N-no," Jessica stuttered. Her grip on Prince Albert's collar tightened, and the retriever yelped.

"I could've sworn he walked right over to you." Ken peered into Jessica's face. "Are you sure he didn't make some kind of crack?"

"He—I—I don't remember," she said weakly.

Ken's eyes blazed. "He did, didn't he?"

Jessica thought as fast and furiously as she could, given her distracted frame of mind. Maybe it would be better to tell him what he wanted to hear. She didn't want him to suspect she was hiding something. If Ken knew what Christian had *really* said—"Meet me at the beach tomorrow morning"—if he knew Christian wasn't some brutal, insulting stranger, but the boy Jessica loved . . .

"I couldn't really hear—I was so upset seeing you fight that I practically blacked out, but I guess he said . . ." Jessica stumbled into what she hoped was a convincing lie. "Something about Sweet Valley guys being losers and I should try somebody from . . . it doesn't matter, Ken." She put a hand on his arm. "It's over."

Ken's whole body was taut with restrained fury. "No, it's not over," he declared, pulling Jessica close and pressing her against his chest. "He's not going to get away with harassing you like that. I can't believe I just left you there. What if he'd—"

"But nothing happened. He took off like everybody else." Jessica's voice trembled. "Let's drop it. I just want to forget about tonight."

"But look at you." Ken cupped her face in his hands. "You're shaking like a leaf. And me . . ." Anger flickered in his eyes. "We can't forget tonight. *I* can't. Not if I have any pride. Next chance I get, I'm putting that Palisades punk in his place. He'll be sorry he even looked at you."

"You—you mean you're going to fight him . . . them . . . again?"

"There's unfinished business, Jess," said Ken. "We'd be a bunch of gutless wimps if we didn't want to take them on again, some time and some place where the police won't barge in."

Jessica stared at Ken, at the bruises, the swollen lip. Dried blood darkened his chin like razor stubble, making him look as if he'd been in a war. "War," she said aloud, remembering Elizabeth's words. "That's what this is."

Ken nodded somberly. "And Sweet Valley's going to win. I promise you that."

Jessica lowered her head against his chest so she wouldn't have to meet his eyes. To Ken things were so simple, so black and white. Sweet Valley High versus Palisades High, us versus them, good versus evil. But for her . . .

Either way I lose, Jessica thought, more horrified than ever by her position. Her relationship with Ken and her illicit love for Christian had landed her smack in the middle of the high school war.

Elizabeth was about to turn out the light when the phone on her nightstand rang. She picked it up quickly. "Hello?"

"Liz, it's me," her boyfriend's familiar voice said.

"Todd! Where are you?"

"Patman's, but I'm heading home. Can I swing by your house on the way?"

It was late, but Elizabeth decided she couldn't wait until the next day to hear the whole story from Todd in person. "My parents are asleep, so we'll have to be quiet," she cautioned. "Just let yourself in the side door."

Ten minutes later they were curled up on the

den sofa with cups of hot lemon-scented tea. Every time Elizabeth looked at Todd's bruised and swollen jaw, she winced. "Do you want an ice pack?" she asked.

Todd shook his head, grinning wryly. "I know I'm a gruesome sight, but it's really not as bad as it looks."

Elizabeth couldn't believe he was smiling. *It's like he had a good time tonight!* she thought in amazement. Out loud, she asked, "So how did it start?"

"They came up to us at the dance, a bunch of Palisades guys—mostly from the football team. You know McMullen, the linebacker? He started in about the game the other day, taunting Ken about losing. Matthews was cool for a minute or two. Just told the guy to get lost. But then a few of the other Palisades guys started dumping on Sweet Valley, and naturally we said a few things back. Out of nowhere one of their guys shoved Aaron, and it looked like we were going to get into it right then and there. Bruce suggested we go outside to settle the question."

Elizabeth shuddered. "I don't get it. Why did you have to fight? Why couldn't you just walk away from each other?"

Todd looked at her as if she'd just asked the stupidest question in the history of the world. "Because you don't walk away in a situation like that, Liz. We couldn't let those Palisades bums brag about how they beat us in football and trashed our yards and then not do anything to stand up for ourselves."

"But the rest of us were trying to have fun," said Elizabeth. "We worked hard planning that dance and—"

"And it was a crummy idea," Todd interrupted. "I told you that right from the beginning. Why would we want to party with Palisades?"

"Tons of people came," Elizabeth countered. "We made hundreds of dollars to give to charity."

"Because you turned the dance into a competition by saying whichever school had the biggest turnout would get to give all the proceeds to the charity of its choice. A competition," Todd repeated emphatically. "That's the only way you're ever going to get Sweet Valley and Palisades together—in a battle of some sort."

Elizabeth didn't want to argue the point now. Lifting a hand, she tentatively touched Todd's face. "I'm just so *mad*. Because you guys ruined the dance and because . . . because I was scared," she admitted. "Jessica fainted and someone splattered blood all over her, and for all I knew, you were hurt. I mean, things got rough, and they could've got rougher! What if someone had pulled a knife or a gun or something?"

Todd wrapped his muscular arms around her

and pulled her close. "No one pulled a knife or a gun, and no one got seriously hurt. A few black eyes—nothing that won't heal in a day or two."

"The bumps and bruises will heal," said Elizabeth, "but the rivalry with Palisades won't, will it?"

"It's worse than ever," Todd admitted grimly. "We got the worst of it in this scrap tonight, and we're all thinking in terms of revenge."

Elizabeth snuggled closer, wishing she never had to leave the safety of Todd's arms. At the same time, the tender moment felt a little strange, given what had taken place earlier that evening. *How could he be punching out some guy one minute and holding me the next?* she wondered. "Revenge," she said. "What a terrible word."

"Depends on how you look at it," Todd replied. "I'm psyched to pay Palisades back for tonight. Everybody's psyched."

"You mean, every *guy*. Most of the girls have a different attitude."

"As long as you *try* to see it from our point of view." Todd drew back to look deep into her eyes. "As long as we're all on the same side."

"Of course we're on the same side," Elizabeth assured him. But she couldn't help thinking about Marla and Caitlin. Were they with *their* boyfriends at this very moment, listening to a different version of the same story? Were their boyfriends forcing them to prove their loyalty? Now that the school rivalry had escalated to an all-out war, would the Sweet Valley and Palisades girls be able to remain friends?

The sky was still dark with just the faintest rim of pink in the east when Jessica crawled out of bed and began silently to dress in a swimsuit, shorts, a T-shirt, and sports sandals. She hadn't slept a wink, but her body felt taut and electrified. She'd kept her surfing a secret from everyone but Lila, so she crept downstairs, careful not to wake her parents or Elizabeth. A few minutes later, with her hot pink wet suit and her brother's old surfboard in the back of the Jeep, Jessica was speeding along empty streets toward the Pacific.

As she neared the beach, she lifted her foot slightly from the gas pedal and let the Jeep coast more slowly. All at once she was shivering, both from the cool morning air blowing in the window and from apprehension. *Will he really be there?* she wondered. In the first misty, blushing light of morning, it was easy to believe that it had all been a dream: her surfing lessons, the rumble at the dance the night before, even Christian himself. Jessica thought about Ken's concern for her, and his explosive anger and desire for revenge. If he ever found out the truth . . .

Maybe I should do a U-turn and drive back home, she told herself.

But she continued north on the coast highway until she reached the last Sweet Valley town beach. At this early hour there was only one other vehicle in the small municipal lot: Christian's old powder blue VW van. At the sight of it, her heart somersaulted. Jessica parked the Jeep next to the van, then hauled out the surfboard, balancing it on her head as she crossed the dunes, her feet digging into the cool, damp sand.

As always, the sight and sound and smell of the vast ocean took Jessica's breath away. Waves rolled into shore, crashing rhythmically—she felt their power vibrating up through the soles of her feet. Standing the surfboard on its nose in the sand, she looked around the deserted beach. "Christian?" she whispered, her voice lost in the sound of wind and waves.

He emerged from the shadow of a dune, his tall, athletic body a dark silhouette against the dawn sky. Ordinarily, he would have run to her, seized her in his arms, and whirled her in a dizzy, laughing circle. This morning was different. *They* were different—not the same carefree young lovers they used to be.

As she looked into Christian's sober, unsmiling face, Jessica recalled her last glimpse of him: the previous night, as she'd crumpled half fainting behind the warehouse. *He goes to Palisades High,* she reminded herself. *He punched Ken. He was right in the middle of the fight—one of the guys who started it, maybe.*

Christian stepped closer, and a sea of conflicting emotions surged in Jessica's heart. She didn't know whether she wanted to hug him or hit him or both. Then she gazed into his eyes and saw the hope and love behind the sorrow and uncertainty. "Jessica?" Christian said, a question in his low, husky voice.

Tears brimming, Jessica rushed forward into his arms. She buried her face against his chest, and for a long moment they clung to each other as if they were drowning. Finally Christian pulled back so he could look at her. "Jess, if I'd known you went to Sweet Valley High . . ."

His voice trailed off. Jessica sniffled. "Would it have made a difference? You wouldn't have offered to teach me how to surf? You wouldn't have . . ." *Fallen in love with me?* she finished silently.

Christian stroked her cheek with the back of his hand. "I don't see how I could've stayed away from you, but . . . it's awkward."

Jessica managed a weak smile. "That's the understatement of the century!"

"I suppose you know the Sweet Valley guys who were in the fight."

She nodded. "Sure. I go to school with them. They're my friends."

"When you came outside and saw me," Christian said, studying her tearstained face, "I was fighting with a guy from the football team—the quarterback. Matthews. Is *he* a friend of yours?"

So far Ken had fallen for all of her lies, and he was still in the dark about Christian. Was there any point in lying to Christian, though? "He's more than a friend," Jessica confessed. "He's my boyfriend."

Christian had been holding her, but now his arms dropped to his sides. For a minute they stood face-to-face, both struggling to comprehend the horrible, twisted complexity of the situation. "It's—it's over, isn't it?" Jessica stammered at last, a sob catching in her throat. "We can't go on like this now . . . now that we *know*."

Christian sat down abruptly, his head in his hands. Jessica knew what he was going to say before he said it, but even so, the words cut like a knife. "We should never see each other again."

Jessica's knees buckled. She, too, crumpled to the sand. "Never?"

Christian lifted dull, hopeless eyes to hers, not answering. *Never,* Jessica repeated to herself. The word was like a prison sentence pronounced by a merciless judge. *Never, never, never . . .*

Chapter 3

"A special assembly. Gee, I wonder what *this* could be about?" Sweet Valley High junior Maria Santelli said dryly as she and her boyfriend, Winston Egbert, joined the river of students flowing into the auditorium before school on Monday.

"There was no way Chrome Dome wouldn't find out about the police breaking up the fight at the dance," Winston commented as he dropped into a seat near the rear of the auditorium. "That's big news in a town like Sweet Valley."

"You guys acted like animals, so now we all have to sit through a lecture," sniffed Maria's fellow cheerleader Amy Sutton, tossing her shoulder-length blond hair as she scooted into the row behind Winston and Maria. "Isn't there a more civilized way to settle a disagreement than pounding each other to a pulp?"

"You chicks just don't understand," Bruce Patman put in as he draped himself over a seat next to Amy.

Amy balled up her fist and shook it at him playfully. "Call me a chick one more time, and I'll prove you're not the only one with a mean right hook."

"Testosterone," drawled Lila Fowler, brushing imaginary lint off her chair before sitting down. "The root of all evil."

"But the world wouldn't be much fun without it," Winston rejoined with a wink.

"It's so pointless to fight, though. What does it prove?" Maria hooked her arm through Winston's and rested her head on his shoulder. "I'm just glad you didn't get hurt."

Winston's face reddened slightly. Bruce had accused him of cowardice the other night, and the other guys, wearing their own scrapes and bruises like badges of honor, were still ribbing him about his unmarked appearance. *Just because I didn't get my nose busted doesn't mean I'm a wimp,* Winston reasoned with himself. *Does it?*

The auditorium filled up quickly. Jessica, Elizabeth, Todd, Aaron, Heather Mallone, Bill Chase, and DeeDee Gordon filed into the row in front of Winston just as Mr. Cooper, the bald principal of Sweet Valley High, approached the podium onstage.

"I'll keep this short and sweet," Mr. Cooper

announced when the buzz of voices quieted down. "I was advised by the chief of police of the disturbance at the dance Friday night. I don't know the names of the individuals responsible, but I'm very disappointed that a small group would cause such trouble for the student body at large."

Bruce blew a raspberry and Winston stifled a guffaw.

"I called an emergency meeting with Mrs. Chang, the Palisades High principal," Mr. Cooper continued, "and we agreed that the rivalry has got out of hand. It's time for both schools to take action to put an end to it."

"I'll put an end to it," muttered Bruce, "when I break Greg McMullen's face."

"For the next month," boomed Mr. Cooper, "and longer if necessary, no one is to wear school colors except to athletic events."

There were mutters of protest. Winston jumped to his feet and pounded the chest of his red-and-white Gladiators sweatshirt. "You mean *this* is illegal?" he yelped with comic melodrama.

Mr. Cooper didn't join in the laughter that bubbled through the auditorium. "No school colors except at games," he repeated sternly. "That includes shorts, T-shirts, sweats, caps, and letter jackets."

Winston dropped back into his seat, shaking his

head in disbelief. "We're just proud of our school, we're not gangsters," he mumbled to Maria.

"I think it's a good idea," she replied. "Things need to quiet down."

"Yeah, but we're talking about freedom of expression," Winston argued. "If I want to wear—"

"Ssh." Maria jabbed him with her elbow.

Chrome Dome was still laying down the law. "In the interest of fostering better relations between Sweet Valley High and Palisades High, a task force of students from both schools will be formed to come up with a goodwill strategy. Anyone interested in volunteering can see me after the assembly."

"Goodwill between Sweet Valley and Palisades," Bruce sneered. "Yeah, when pigs fly."

"When cows windsurf," Winston added.

"When horses skydive," Todd contributed.

Mr. Cooper had paused in his speech. Something about the principal's solemn posture made Winston sit up a little straighter. "Finally," said Mr. Cooper, his words forceful and deliberate, "if I find evidence of anyone making trouble in the name of school spirit, that student will be suspended from school. If the offense is grievous enough, that student will be permanently expelled."

A stunned silence fell over the auditorium. *Expelled,* Winston thought, gulping. *As in kicked out for good. As in no graduation, no diploma, no college, no career, no life.*

He shot a glance at Bruce, who was nonchalantly checking his wristwatch. Todd had a defiant, stubborn expression on his face. "They're not buying it," Winston whispered. He realized he was squeezing Maria's fingers and loosened his grip. "They're not intimidated by Chrome Dome."

"Who?" Maria asked.

He kept his voice low so no one but his girlfriend could hear him. "Patman and Wilkins and the rest. They're not going to back off. Chrome Dome's threats won't cool things off—if anything, it'll be worse. It's like a dare."

Maria raised her slender dark eyebrows. "What do you mean?"

"It's like drawing a line in the sand and telling someone not to cross it," Winston explained. "You know that person will jump across it the moment you turn your back."

"You really don't think they'll listen to reason?" she asked.

Winston recalled the discussion at the abandoned warehouse Friday night. Not that you could have called it a "discussion," with all that yelling about justice and revenge. Reason had nothing to do with this. "Wars don't end just like that"—Winston snapped his fingers—"just because one person—some third party—says so."

Maria shook her head. "What I don't get is how this turned into a war in the first place."

Winston didn't entirely understand, either. "Sweet Valley's out for blood," he told Maria. "Even guys like Todd and Ken, who are usually pretty levelheaded. You should've heard them the other night, talking about bashing heads."

"Maybe they'll be satisfied with talking about it. The weekend was pretty quiet, after Friday night."

"The calm before the storm," said Winston, his tone dire. "Don't be fooled."

The assembly lasted five more minutes as the vice principal made a few general announcements. Winston didn't hear a word. He strained his ears trying to listen in on what Bruce was saying to Todd, Aaron, and Bill. He couldn't quite catch it, but he had a hunch he knew the general subject matter: how to wipe Palisades High School off the map.

Things seemed about to spin wildly out of control, and there was nothing he could do to stop it. *We could get into some serious trouble*, Winston thought. *Suspended from school—or expelled. Forget that.* He looked at Bruce, Bill, Aaron, and Todd, still sporting purplish abrasions from Friday night's brawl. *We could get killed!*

Winston sighed. He knew his friends were serious

about getting revenge on Palisades, and he also knew he'd be by their side every step of the way. Wasn't that what friendship was all about?

"Tell me you didn't just volunteer for the task force," Todd said to Elizabeth as they left the auditorium.

After the assembly she'd run down to the front of the auditorium to exchange a few words with the principal. Now she lifted her eyebrows at Todd's snide, disapproving tone. "As a matter of fact, I did. Do you have a problem with that?"

"I can't believe you're going to be one of Chrome Dome's enforcers!" Todd said.

"I'm not going to be an enforcer!" Elizabeth declared, indignant. "The point is to open up a line of communication. I think it's a good idea."

"What happened to our being on the same side?" Todd challenged. "You could at least be neutral, Liz."

"I *am* on your side, but I never said I was neutral. I'm a newspaper columnist, remember?" Elizabeth elbowed her boyfriend in the ribs, trying to lighten up the mood. "So I guess you won't be wearing that shirt for a while," she teased.

Todd looked down at his gray T-shirt, emblazoned on the chest with a maroon "SVH." "Are you kidding?" His tone was still belligerent. "Chrome Dome doesn't scare me."

"But it's a school rule now. No red and white."

Todd shrugged. "Rules are made to be broken—that's my motto."

She couldn't help laughing at Todd's new rebel-without-a-cause pose. "Since when? Anyhow, what purpose does it serve? If we want to have peace—"

"Peace with those jerks?" Todd exclaimed fiercely. "No way. The task force can do its thing, but that doesn't mean the rest of the school will go along with it."

Elizabeth placed her hands on her hips. "You mean you're not even going to try?"

"Look, Palisades started it. And it's not like we're in this for our own glory. We're defending our school's honor. *And* protecting our women," Todd added, running a hand up her arm and giving her what she thought was an incredibly patronizing smile.

Elizabeth shook off his hand indignantly. "I don't need protection, thank you very much. You should hear yourself. You sound like some macho minibrain!"

"And you sound like a self-righteous—" Todd bit off his sentence. "Sorry, Liz. Why are *we* fighting? The fight's with Palisades."

"But that's just my point!" The discussion was going in circles, and Elizabeth literally felt dizzy. "Why does there have to be a fight at all?"

Todd shook his head, as if he couldn't believe her denseness. "Maybe it is a guy thing, Liz," he said. "Maybe nothing I say is going to help you understand. In which case, maybe you should just stand aside and let us handle it."

"Stand aside and let *you* handle it? What, because I'm a *girl*?" Elizabeth rubbed her temples, which were suddenly throbbing. "This is the most infuriating conversation I've ever had in my entire life."

The bell rang, signaling three minutes until the start of first-period classes. "Well, relax, it's over," murmured Todd, dropping a kiss on her cheek. "And I won."

"You didn't win and it's not over!" she declared, stomping off in the direction of her locker.

"See you at lunch!" Todd called after her.

But at lunch Elizabeth was still seething over her argument with Todd. Instead of going to the cafeteria, she headed to the newspaper office with Penny Ayala, editor in chief of *The Oracle* and one of Elizabeth's closest friends. "I mean, it was almost embarrassing," Elizabeth told Penny, shifting her notebooks from one arm to the other. "He went on and on about its basically being the guys' duty to keep feuding with Palisades to defend the honor of Sweet Valley High and protect their women. He actually *said* that: 'Protect our women.' Can you believe it?"

Penny rolled her eyes. "Unfortunately, I can. Neil's talking the exact same way." Penny dated Neil Freemount, a cute junior on the tennis team.

Elizabeth tossed her blond ponytail. "Is it absurd or what?"

"It's almost laughable," agreed Penny, "but the bottom line is they're still talking about fighting. It's like the kind of thing that goes on in the city. Gang warfare or something. If you hadn't called the police the other night . . ."

"There are so many *ifs*." Elizabeth bit her lip. "For instance, if we hadn't organized the dance in the first place. But we can't go back in time and undo what's already done." They reached the *Oracle* office. Penny unlocked the door. "What I *can* do," Elizabeth went on, her tone determined, "is keep trying to have an effect on what's still to come."

She sat down in front of one of the computer terminals and began typing furiously. "An editorial?" asked Penny, glancing over from her own computer screen.

"Yep," Elizabeth confirmed. "Todd says I don't understand and that I should just stay out of it. But this is my school, too, and I love it. I want peace, and I know in their hearts pretty much everyone else does, too."

She'd already written half a page when the

office phone rang. Penny picked it up, then handed the receiver to Elizabeth. "It's for you."

The caller identified herself. "Liz, it's Marla."

"Marla!" exclaimed Elizabeth. She hadn't spoken to her friend since the night of the dance. "Are things as crazy at PH as they are here?"

The girls traded stories. "We had a special assembly this morning, too," said Marla. "No school colors, the whole deal. And supposedly the mayor's even talking about a curfew for teenagers if there are any more incidents!"

"A curfew!" Elizabeth whistled. "That's intense."

"So I joined the task force, and I'm also writing an editorial asking kids to come together for peace," Marla said. "I kind of feel responsible, since the dance was my idea and that's when things started to get out of hand. It's the least I can do, you know?"

"Yeah," said Elizabeth. "I feel the same way."

"Good luck."

"You, too."

Elizabeth hung up the phone and resumed typing with increased fervor. "Come together for peace," she murmured out loud, her spirits lifting. It sounded so easy—all that was needed was a change of direction. "'Put your energy and school spirit to good use,'" Elizabeth typed. "'Let's build up Sweet Valley High instead of tearing it down.

We can be proud of our community without trashing our neighbors.'"

As the words poured out, Elizabeth felt renewed optimism. Peace made perfect sense, and she was confident that as soon as they read her editorial, her fellow students—even Todd and Bruce and the rest of the boys—would see it her way.

"So when you walked outside, the fight was still in full swing." Amy leaned across the lunch table, her gray eyes glittering with curiosity. "I heard this really huge Palisades guy was totally pummeling Ken. Was it someone from the football team?"

Jessica poked at her chef's salad. "I didn't really get a good look at him," she mumbled.

Lila tapped her long red fingernails on the table. "What about that Greg McMullen guy, the totally hot Palisades linebacker? He's the one who started the whole thing, socking Ken after the football game. I bet he was smack in the middle of the fight. Did you see him? Was he decking people right and left?"

Jessica shrugged. "I don't remember."

"C'mon," Amy cajoled. "We want details. You must have noticed something. I mean, you got splattered all over with blood, didn't you?"

Jessica felt her stomach heave and she pushed

her plate away. "Don't you two have anything better to think about?"

Amy glanced at Lila. "Do we?"

"Not really," Lila answered.

"Well, sorry to disappoint you, but it was dark. I saw—" Jessica caught herself before saying the name "Christian." "I saw that big guy punch Ken, and then I passed out. When I opened my eyes again, everyone had taken off."

Amy sighed. "I wish I'd been there. This probably sounds kinky, but I think guys getting all sweaty and panting and punching each other is kind of sexy."

"You are so deviant, Ms. Sutton," Lila said with a smile, "but I have to agree with you. And the way everyone's talking, there's going to be another huge fight any day now. The fight to end all fights, to decide once and for all which school is number one."

Jessica fought back the urge to launch out of her seat and sprint from the cafeteria. There was no point running—she wouldn't escape the gossip, the rumors, the morbid relish with which everyone discussed the fight and its aftermath. All the girls wanted to hear Jessica's eyewitness version of what had happened. *It's sick,* she thought, *getting a thrill from blood and guts and violence.*

Just then she felt a hand on the back of her neck.

She jumped, a strangled cry squeaking from her throat. "Didn't mean to scare you," said Ken, massaging her neck lightly as he dropped into the empty chair next to her.

Jessica's skin crawled at Ken's touch. He'd draped his arm firmly across her shoulders, and it was all she could do not to squirm out of his grasp. In an effort to distract herself, she focused on Bruce, who'd taken a seat between Amy and Lila. "What did you ladies think about Chrome Dome's speech?" Bruce asked.

"He sounded serious," replied Amy, twisting the lid off a bottle of fruit juice.

"The fun's over," Lila agreed.

Bruce cocked an eyebrow at Ken. "I'd say the fun's just beginning, wouldn't you, Matthews?"

Ken's muscular arm tightened around Jessica. His whole body felt tense with anticipation. "We're not through with Palisades," Ken said. "Far from it."

Bruce's eyes gleamed. "And when we are . . ."

"Those punks won't dare show their faces in Sweet Valley ever again," Ken concluded.

Lila and Amy appeared thrilled by this declaration, but Jessica's heart sank into her sandals. She pictured a future confrontation between the Sweet Valley and Palisades boys—bodies boxing in a black back alley, fists flying, blood flowing. Only this time it was Ken punching Christian—Christian, who was hurt and bleeding.

Even though she and Christian had decided to sacrifice their love, she couldn't help feeling afraid for him. She'd stayed away from the beach for two mornings in a row, all the while wondering if *he* was able to stay away or if he'd gone there looking for her. Jessica couldn't help hoping, deep in her secret heart, that she'd see Christian again—and be with him.

Chapter 4

Curious to see who else had joined the committee, Elizabeth looked around as she entered the classroom where the first task-force meeting was being held on Monday after school. A dozen Sweet Valley High students, representing all four grades, were already seated.

Elizabeth slipped into a desk in the front row by the window. She flashed a smile at popular sophomores Jade Wu and David Prentiss. "It's good to see you guys here," she greeted them.

Jade and David were both thoughtful, creative people—Jade was a talented dancer and David was an artist. "We'll probably get some flack from some people," said graceful, almond-eyed Jade, "but my conscience would bug me if I didn't speak out on this issue."

Elizabeth nodded sympathetically. Then she twisted in her chair to wave to A.J. Morgan. A.J. played basketball with Todd, and he'd dated Jessica way back when. "I know what you're thinking, Liz," A.J. said with an easy grin. "Wilkins and the rest of the team are going to give me a lot of grief. I'm supposed to be talking tough, snapping towels in the locker room and all that. But I don't mind telling them and everybody else that I think we should take the rivalry back to the basketball court and football field."

"Good speech, A.J."

They all turned to see who'd spoken. Mr. Collins, the adviser to the student newspaper and Elizabeth's favorite English teacher, had just stepped into the room. Ms. Dalton, the vivacious, attractive French instructor, was right behind him. Elizabeth was glad to see that they were the faculty appointed to the task force—they were both young and well liked, in tune with the many moods of the diverse student body.

Mr. Collins hitched himself up onto the edge of the desk at the front of the classroom. "I hope you'll repeat it when we meet with our counterparts from Palisades High."

"Sure," said A.J. "I mean, it's how I feel."

"But it's not necessarily a popular opinion right now," Mr. Collins said. A few more students drifted in, including Penny and Enid. Mr. Collins fixed them all with his piercing blue eyes. "It's not cool. They're going to accuse you of being a coward and a wimp."

"What are you getting at?" asked Dana Larson, the lead singer for The Droids. She ran a hand through her cropped blond hair. "It's almost like you're trying to talk us out of this."

"Just testing, Dana." Mr. Collins's handsome face creased in a smile. "Just making sure you're committed. Because it's not easy swimming against the tide."

As if to illustrate his point, at that instant the door to the classroom banged open. Elizabeth glimpsed a blur of bodies and faces running past in the corridor. "Traitors!" someone hollered. "Weasels! Why don't you just transfer to Palisades?"

There were a few more insulting shouts. Ms. Dalton crossed quickly to the door and looked out. "They're gone," she said. "Now, *that's* cowardly. If they've got something to say, they should say it openly, to our faces." She closed the door again.

Jade, David, and some of the other students looked distinctly uncomfortable. Elizabeth knew her own face mirrored their dismay. "That's what's in store for us," said Mr. Collins, laughing at their expressions. "But don't worry, it won't be all bad. I bet you'll be surprised how many kids secretly agree with you. They'll be coming out of the woodwork to thank you for taking a stand on their behalf."

"When do we get started?" Elizabeth asked. "And *how* do we get started?"

"We begin tomorrow afternoon, at Palisades," Ms. Dalton replied. "As for how, I think the best way is to do exactly what we've been doing here today. Talk. Express our feelings. Ask questions."

When the meeting was over, Elizabeth walked to the *Oracle* office with Penny to help the other staff members get the next issue of the paper ready for the printers. "I'm psyched about the task force," said Penny. "I bet it'll make a big difference. I mean, of course there are people who'll never come around, like those bozos who heckled us. But luckily most of the kids at this school aren't such total jerks."

Elizabeth hoped Penny didn't notice the embarrassed blush tinting her cheeks. She had high expectations for the task force, too, but at the moment she was preoccupied by something else. Elizabeth wouldn't bet her life on it, but she thought she recognized one of the voices—one of those "bozos" had been her boyfriend.

"Aren't you going a little over the top with the secrecy stuff, Patman?" Winston asked that evening.

Bruce had summoned the rest of the Sweet

Valley boys to his house for a strategy meeting. He'd greeted each new arrival by hissing a secret password in his ear, "to be used at all future meetings." Now, after herding them into the mansion's enormous rec room, Bruce was running around closing blinds and pulling curtains.

"Yeah," said Ken. "You can't really think Palisades is planning to *spy* on us."

"Better safe than sorry," Bruce insisted, dimming the lights.

Ken flopped onto one of the L-shaped leather sofas. "Let's make this quick, OK? I've got a date."

Bruce frowned. "We'll take as long as we need. This should be your top priority, Matthews."

Ken shrugged. It wasn't worth arguing—Bruce was running the show. But Ken was starting to wonder if they weren't taking this revenge business in the wrong direction. He'd felt pretty stupid that afternoon, galloping past the task-force committee shouting rude names.

"So this is the way I see it." Bruce paced back and forth in front of them like a military commander inspecting his troops. "We should look at it like a football game, right, Matthews? Palisades is a pretty tough adversary, they may have a few points on us, but this is just the first quarter. We can outsmart them—we've got guts and brains and a damned good quarterback."

He stabbed a finger at Ken. "So what's our first move?"

Ken realized that everyone was waiting for him to say something. The quarterback was supposed to have the game plan, after all. For the first time in his life, Ken almost wished he were someone else—Winston Egbert, maybe, someone with the freedom to clown around. *They expect me to throw a touchdown pass,* he thought. *I can't afford to fumble. I've got to uphold my image.*

"You're the captain of this particular team, Patman," Ken said, "but I can tell you that the key to success on the field is taking the other guys by surprise. They think you're heading one way, and you end up rushing in the opposite direction. We want to catch Palisades with their guard down."

Ken wasn't really thinking about what he was saying, but apparently his offhand remark struck a chord. The rest of the guys all started yammering at once. An hour later they were primed for action even though they hadn't made much headway figuring out the nitty-gritty details of their revenge scheme. Bruce led them in one last chant of "Pulverize Palisades" before they all headed off.

Ken gave Aaron a ride home. "What do you think about all this?" he asked, hoping Aaron would admit to having mixed feelings about the plan to step up the hostilities against Palisades.

But Aaron seemed 100 percent enthusiastic.

"We've got to do what we've got to do," he declared, as gung ho as a new army recruit.

"Right," said Ken.

After dropping Aaron off, Ken drove in pensive silence, wondering what had come over him. *I should be totally up for this, like Aaron, like Bruce. What's holding me back all of a sudden?* As he turned onto Calico Drive, it struck him. Jessica. She was still acting spooked, and he felt rotten, knowing she was scared because of what he'd done. Her reaction to the whole situation served as a not-so-flattering mirror. It gave Ken another view of his and the rest of the guys' behavior.

"All that garbage about how the war with Palisades is like a football game. It's *not* a football game—that's just it," Ken said out loud. Maybe they should have left the rivalry on the playing field. After all, he was a quarterback, not a thug.

He pulled up at the curb in front of Jessica's house. Striding up the walk to the Wakefields' front door, Ken suddenly wanted nothing more than to forget all about the war with Palisades High and hold Jessica in his arms. Sure, the idea of battle could be intoxicating, and Bruce was working hard at keeping all the guys fired up. But Jessica mattered more than all that. He was supposed to take care of her, and in turn, she'd take care of him. Her love would keep him grounded and sane, as it always had.

He rang the doorbell. Mr. Wakefield opened the door. "Hello, Ken. Come on in," invited the tall, dark-haired attorney. "Jess is in the den, I think."

Ken found Jessica curled up on the couch with an afghan wrapped around her legs. When she saw Ken, she pointed the remote control at the television and switched it off. "Hi," she said without much enthusiasm.

Ken sat down next to her. "How about going for a drive?" he suggested, bending to brush her cheek with a kiss. "Miller's Point, maybe?"

Jessica shrugged. "I guess I'd rather stick around here."

"Fine with me, as long as you don't think anyone'll walk in," he teased.

Jessica shrugged again. "They're all off doing stuff. No one will bother us."

"Good." Ken wrapped his arms around her and pulled her close. "Because I've been thinking that maybe you need some extra attention."

He brought his mouth close to hers and closed his eyes in anticipation of a long, warm kiss. Instead, Jessica turned her head so that his lips landed on her ear. "What's the matter?" he asked.

"I just don't want to . . . your lip." She pointed. "It's still puffed up from the fight. I don't want to hurt you."

"Hey, this is the way to make it better," coaxed Ken. "Don't you want to heal me?"

Jessica inched away from him on the sofa. "Seriously. It looks terrible. It must hurt like crazy. Why don't we take it easy?"

She thinks I'm a wimp, that I got the worst of it in the fight with that guy from Palisades, Ken thought. "It doesn't hurt that much," he snapped, his temper flaring. "You don't have to treat me like an invalid!"

"I wasn't!" Jessica protested. "It's just, if we kiss, it might start bleeding again."

"I've had cuts and bruises plenty of times before from games, and you haven't been turned off then," Ken said accusingly.

Jessica blushed slightly. "I'm not turned off," she hurried to assure him, patting his arm as if that could make up for not wanting to kiss him. "I'm just trying to be considerate."

After silently counting to ten in his head, Ken felt a lot calmer. But a renewed hunger for revenge had taken root. "Sorry I got ticked off, Jess," he apologized. "I have all this pent-up energy, you know? I'm dying to get a lock on that clown from Palisades, grind his face in the dirt." Ken punched his right fist into the palm of his left hand with a loud smack. "After I get that out of my system, I'll be back to my old self."

Jessica's eyes were large in her pale face. "Why do you have to get even?" she asked, her voice shaking. "Why go out of your way to get into another fight?"

"What do you mean?"

"That maybe you should keep away from Palisades. Can't you talk Bruce and the rest of the gang into just letting it go?"

An hour earlier Ken might have considered Jessica's plea reasonable. But now he found himself reading between the lines, and he didn't like the message that was coming across. He didn't like it one bit. "You think we can't beat those guys. You think if we tangle with them again, they'll come out on top."

"I didn't say—"

"I can't let that Palisades jerk get away with this." Ken gestured to the bruised lip that Jessica had refused to kiss. "What kind of man would I be if I didn't stand up for myself?"

Jessica's eyes brimmed with tears. "I'm just . . . scared," she whispered.

Ken pulled her close, cradling her against his chest. Driving over to her house earlier, he'd been wondering himself if stepping up the war against Palisades High was really the right thing to do. Now he knew without a doubt that it was. "I've got to get even with that guy if I'm going to respect myself," he murmured into Jessica's silky blond hair. *And if you're going to respect me*, he silently added.

As Ken walked to his car, Jessica stood on the front step and blew him a kiss. Then she stepped back into the house and closed the door, sighing wearily. It used to be so easy and fun to be alone with Ken. Kissing and cuddling with him had been her favorite thing to do in the world. But tonight she was worn out from playing the role of the loving, supportive girlfriend because she didn't *feel* loving in her heart. *Did he notice?* she wondered as she climbed the stairs to the second floor. *Probably I shouldn't have made such a big deal out of kissing him, or rather,* not *kissing him. It would've been safer just to do it. It wouldn't have killed me.*

But ever since she'd kissed Christian for the first time, her physical feelings for Ken had gone stone cold. It was getting more and more painful to pretend she loved him as much as ever, and at the same time more and more impossible to imagine breaking up with him, telling him honestly that she'd met someone else. She and Ken had been a serious couple for a while—it was one of the longest relationships of her life. His affection for her ran deep, and she knew he'd be devastated. And how would he react when she added, "Oh, by the way, you may be seeing me around town with your archenemy from Palisades—that's who I'm dating now"?

But it won't happen that way, Jessica told herself glumly. Why would Christian want to go out with her, even if she were free? After all, she lived in Sweet Valley. If Ken and Christian were enemies, then so by rights were Christian and Jessica.

"What a hideous, tangled mess," she moaned out loud.

"Is that you, Jess?" Elizabeth called from her bedroom. "Are you talking to me?"

Jessica paused in the hall outside Elizabeth's half-open door, all at once overcome by the desire to confess her predicament to her sister. Elizabeth was always so practical and clearheaded. *She'll be shocked, but she'll help me see a way out of this,* Jessica thought, buoyed by sudden hope.

"Can I come in, Liz?"

"Sure."

Jessica pushed open the door to her sister's room. Elizabeth was seated at her desk, tapping on her computer keyboard. "You're up late. Working on an article for the newspaper?" Jessica asked, flopping onto the neatly made twin bed.

Elizabeth moved the mouse to delete a phrase, typed in something else, and then deleted that, too. Finally, with a sigh, she quit the program and turned off the computer. "It's a poem," she admitted, "and not a very good one. There's this one image—I just can't get the words right."

Jessica wasn't interested in talking about poetic imagery. "Liz," she began, "I have to tell you something."

Elizabeth tipped her head to one side. "Yeah?"

"Something I've been doing, on the sly. Something . . . dangerous." Jessica took a deep breath. "The last week or so, I've been—on the beach, I—" She stuttered to a stop.

"What?" pressed Elizabeth, her eyes round with curiosity.

"I . . ." *I met someone from Palisades. We fell in love.* "I've been teaching myself how to surf."

Elizabeth blinked. "To surf? You're kidding!"

"No, I'm not. Lila kind of dared me. We have a bet that I won't win this surfing competition and a trip to Hawaii and get interviewed on Rock TV. I mean, she says I won't. So I've been going to the beach really early every morning to practice. Using Steven's old board, you know? And I was going to keep it a secret until I won the competition. But then I thought maybe . . ." Jessica shrugged, lost in the maze of her own babbling. "I guess I thought someone should know. Just in case."

"Wow," said Elizabeth. "That's wild. But, Jess, it *is* dangerous to surf without a partner. Are there other people on the beach when you go in the morning?"

"There's usually a few other people surfing," Jessica assured her sister. "In fact . . ." *C'mon, say it,* she coached herself. *This is your chance.* But for some reason, now that she was face-to-face with her sister, Jessica couldn't bring herself to talk about Christian. "A couple of times I've got some tips. I've never been alone."

"Good," Elizabeth said. Standing up, she stretched her arms over her head and yawned. "I'm beat. Night, Jess."

"Night, Liz."

Jessica crossed to the bathroom that connected her room to her sister's. After washing up, she stripped off her clothes and slipped on the oversize football shirt she wore as a nightgown, then switched off the light and climbed into bed.

Her window was open and the night breeze rippled the curtains. Jessica stared at the moon shadows dancing on her ceiling. All at once she felt as if she'd just had a very close call. *Thank heavens I didn't tell Liz!* she thought. No one must ever know, not even her twin sister. *I have to forget about Christian,* Jessica counseled herself strictly. Her loyalties should lie with Ken and Sweet Valley High, no question about it. Forget about Christian—it should be easy! After all, in many ways he was still a stranger to her. She knew he went to Palisades High School, and that he had a brother named Jason, but she didn't know anything else—she'd put a stop early on to either of them revealing details about their personal lives.

Jessica closed her eyes. *Easy? No way,* she thought, her throat tight with unshed tears. Maybe she didn't know Christian's address, if he played sports or had any hobbies. But she knew other things. She knew he drove an old powder blue VW van, that he loved surfing, that his deep, husky laughter was deliciously contagious, that the hair curled in an adorable way on the back of his neck when it was wet, that his eyes glowed like stars when he moved close to kiss her . . .

"I'll never forget you, Christian," Jessica whispered to the darkness of her room. "Never."

Chapter 5

She hadn't set her alarm for five A.M. as she had the days when she'd met Christian on the beach for surfing lessons, but on Tuesday Jessica woke up before dawn anyway. For a minute she lay in bed, trying to fall back to sleep. Then she realized it was hopeless. There was no way she'd fall back to sleep . . . and there was no way she could stay away from the beach any longer. She'd avoided it for two whole agonizing days, and now she could feel the ocean drawing her like a magnet. *I have to go,* Jessica thought as she crept around her bedroom in the dark, putting on her bathing suit and packing a backpack with clothes and books for school. *Whether Christian's there or not.*

After waxing Steven's surfboard in the garage, Jessica climbed into the Jeep and released the parking brake, letting it coast silently down the driveway. On the street she started the engine and headed toward the beach.

Three mornings ago, making this same drive, she'd been full of conflicting emotions: anticipation, dread, sorrow, love. This morning was different. There was no suspense, because Christian wouldn't be waiting for her. As she parked the Jeep in the empty lot, any hope she had that the light blue van might be there dissolved.

He's gone from my life, Jessica thought dismally as she trudged toward the water's edge with her board. *Maybe I'll see him someday, at a Sweet Valley–Palisades football game or something, but he'll be sitting on the other side of the stands.* He was out of her life, but he'd left behind an ache, a deep and utter loneliness, that was almost more than Jessica could bear. Where was the pleasure in surfing without Christian?

As soon as she was in the cool water, though, lying flat on her stomach on the board and paddling as Christian had taught her, Jessica started to feel just the tiniest bit better. It was as if Christian were still there with her, carefully watching over and instructing her. The calls of seabirds and the musical splashing of water reminded her of his laughter. The morning sun touched her, as warm as the memory of his love.

Out in deep water, Jessica hitched herself onto

her knees. The waves were big, and for a second she felt a flicker of fear. "Don't be a chicken," she muttered to herself. "You know how to handle them now. Just do what Christian taught you."

But the wave coming at her, rolling across the surface of the ocean at ever-increasing speed, was at least twice as big as any of the ones she'd ridden successfully. Taking a deep breath, Jessica dived underwater, hugging the ocean floor until the wave passed overhead. Then she retrieved her board and scrambled back on top. Dashing the water from her eyes, she waited for another, more manageable wave to come along.

The approaching eight-footer was still on the big side, but she couldn't resist it. *This is crazy,* Jessica thought as she paddled quickly into position and then hopped onto her feet, balancing herself with her arms outstretched. *Crazy . . . but wonderful.* The wave swept her along—it was like flying. She'd never tackled such a tall wave, but she was riding it like a pro. For the first time in days, the blood pumped fast and hot in her veins and she felt alive. If only Christian could see her now!

The wave rushed toward the shore, its momentum subsiding as it foamed onto the sand. The thrill was over. Hopping off her board in the shallows, Jessica waded onto the beach to catch her breath. As she paused to shake out her hair and wipe the salty spray from her face, she glimpsed a small figure, far away at the other end of the beach. Her heart started to thump quickly again.

It's not him, she told herself, bending to flick a strand of seaweed off her leg. *Don't get your hopes up.*

The person was walking in her direction. Now she could see that it was a guy in a cutoff wet suit—tall, lean, tanned, with dark hair. *It can't be,* she thought. *Stop torturing yourself.*

The guy stopped in his tracks and stared in her direction. He was close enough now for her to discern his features. A chill ran up Jessica's spine, and her wet body began to tremble.

It was Christian, and even from a distance she could see the expression of love and longing on his face. He'd come for her, after all.

"I know it's a long book," Mr. Collins said, eyeing the rows of students in his junior English class. "So let's see a show of hands—raise 'em high if you actually made it all the way through *Crime and Punishment.*"

There was a chorus of moans and groans. Winston was one of only a handful of students who admitted to having finished the assignment. "You know what might have worked better, given what everybody's talking about these days, Mr. Collins?"

Winston asked. "Since we're reading Russian stuff, you should have assigned *War and Peace*!"

The rest of the kids in the class cracked up. Mr. Collins grinned. "You're probably right," he conceded. "Well, here's a piece of literature I bet all of you people have read." He tapped a copy of the latest issue of *The Oracle*, which was lying on top of his desk. "Maybe instead of discussing Dostoyevsky, we should talk about the new school rules."

The class murmured agreement to his suggestion. "I'll tell you," said *Oracle* staff member Olivia Davidson, "we've never got so many letters to the editor. A lot of people are really mad about the rules."

"Including me," Ron Edwards proclaimed. "They're taking away our rights, man. Our freedom. Telling us what we can and can't wear, restricting public gatherings and that kind of thing."

"But we need some rules to keep society safe," Elizabeth said. "It's not just supposed to be a punishment."

"We already know what *you* think about this, Liz," Ronnie said sarcastically. "We read the editorial."

Elizabeth narrowed her eyes. "Do you have a point to make, Ronnie?" she asked.

"Yeah," Ronnie replied. "My point is the new rules are stupid, so anybody who agrees with them must be stupid, too."

"Whoa, hold it right there." Mr. Collins raised

his hands. "Let's stay on the subject and not stoop to personal attacks. Take issue with Liz's editorial if you want, Ronnie, but don't criticize her."

"But if we disagree with an opinion, we disagree with the person who expresses it," objected Aaron. "I mean, Liz has to take responsibility for her words. She wrote them, they're hers. So she's got to be prepared to take whatever we throw at her."

"Aaron's right," Elizabeth conceded with a wry smile. "When I wrote the editorial, I knew some people would disagree. That's what it's all about—getting a dialogue started."

"Let's get back to it, then," Mr. Collins said. He pointed at Ronnie. "What I want from you, Mr. Edwards, is argumentative precision. It's not good enough to say something's 'stupid.' Expand on that, please."

Ronnie hunched his shoulders, his posture sullen. "I guess I thought 'stupid' said it all."

"Well, let me see if I can summarize what we've come up with so far," offered Mr. Collins. "Some of us think the new rules are unfair. They limit our freedom of expression. Others feel circumstances justify the rules—we need them to create a safe environment."

Winston raised his hand. "Wasn't it Ben Franklin who said 'Those who would sacrifice their liberty to preserve their safety deserve neither liberty nor safety'? Or something like that."

"Good." Mr. Collins nodded approvingly. "Who wants to comment?"

"We're not giving up our liberty, though," Olivia protested. "Or, OK, just a little bit of it. But aren't we getting sidetracked from what started all this? It was because of a fight. The Bill of Rights doesn't say anything about having the freedom to beat other people up."

The lively debate lasted for the entire period, with the class evenly divided between students in favor of following the new school rules and making peace with Palisades and those opposed. When the bell rang, Ronnie slapped his notebook shut and turned to Winston. "What a waste of time," he drawled. "Like we didn't already know all the girls were bugged about the fighting."

A.J. overheard the remark. "Hey, it's not just girls," he said. "I'm on the task force."

Ronnie gave A.J. an insolent stare. "Like I said, all the girls."

A.J. laughed. "So I'm not a guy because I don't want to rumble with Palisades High."

"If you're not up to it, you're not up to it," said Ronnie. "We can't all be heroes."

"Man, you don't know the first thing *about* heroism," said A.J. "If there's one thing I've learned having a dad in the army it's that you don't shed blood without a really good reason. You don't go to war over nothing. And in the grand scheme of things, this high school rivalry is nothing."

As they filed out of the clasroom, Winston wanted to clap A.J. on the back, but one glance at Ronnie's disapproving expression caused him to zip his lips. *A.J.'s right, though,* Winston thought. A.J. had the courage of his convictions—he didn't hesitate to speak up and take action. He didn't seem worried about the other guys questioning his masculinity—obviously, he was confident and comfortable with himself.

Then there's me. Winston walked down the hallway next to Aaron and Ronnie. *I didn't even have the nerve to tell A.J. I agreed with him because I knew it would make Edwards and Dallas mad. And I don't want to make them mad because I agree with them, too.* Winston scratched his head, confused. How could he be on both sides of the issue at the same time? What was he going to do about the fact that his moral beliefs pulled him in one direction while his loyalty to his friends pulled him in the other?

Todd unwrapped his ham-and-cheese sandwich, glaring at the newspaper lying on the table between him and Elizabeth. "I still can't believe you wrote that."

Before taking a bite of her own turkey-and-alfalfa-sprout sandwich, Elizabeth said coolly, "Well, I did write it and I'm proud of it."

It was lunch period on Tuesday, and throughout the cafeteria Sweet Valley High students continued to discuss the latest issue of *The Oracle*, including Elizabeth's editorial.

"You made me and Bruce and Ken and everybody else out to be bad guys," Todd complained.

"I didn't name any names," protested Elizabeth.

"But everyone knows who you meant."

"So what if they do?" she challenged. "If you guys are fighting a war, you've got to do it in the open and take responsibility."

"You make it sound like we're in it for ourselves, like it doesn't have anything to do with the rest of the school. We're fighting for SVH, Liz."

She shook her head. "Didn't you even listen in Mr. Collins's class today? You're *not* fighting for everybody at SVH. You're not fighting for me—I don't support you at all in this."

Todd's face darkened. "I'm sorry you feel that way, and I'm sorry everybody has to *know* you feel that way. It's sort of embarrassing."

"Embarrassing?"

"Seeing as how you're my girlfriend."

Elizabeth couldn't believe anyone could be so self-centered. "You've got to be kidding. I should shut up about how I feel to keep from *embarrassing* you?"

"You didn't have to splash it all over the newspaper, did you? You didn't have to advertise it."

"I have a right to my own opinion," Elizabeth said hotly. "And I'm not alone. People keep coming up to me to say they agree with me, that they want to cool it with Palisades. Patty Gilbert was just saying that—"

Before she could finish, Todd shoved back his chair. "Look, I've got to run," he announced abruptly, gathering up his trash and tossing it into the nearest bin.

Elizabeth raised her eyebrows. "You're in a hurry all of a sudden," she commented, feeling a little bit hurt. "If you want to change the subject, just say so. You don't have to run away from me."

"It's not that. I really do have a meeting to go to."

"What meeting?"

"Just a meeting," Todd replied unhelpfully. Almost as an afterthought, he dropped a kiss on her cheek. "See ya."

Elizabeth stuffed her half-eaten sandwich back into her lunch bag. With Todd gone, she remembered that she wanted to track down Jessica, who, as far as Elizabeth could tell, had skipped homeroom and all her morning classes. Getting to her feet, Elizabeth scanned the cafeteria. Jessica wasn't sitting with Ken and the guys, or with Lila and Amy at the cheerleading table.

She never made it to school today, Elizabeth concluded, a worried frown creasing her forehead as she hurried out of the cafeteria and headed for the pay phone in the main lobby. When she reached the phone, she stuck in a coin and dialed her own home number. The phone rang four times before the answering machine picked up. It was Jessica's peppy prerecorded voice. "You've reached the Wakefield residence. We can't take your call right now, but if you leave a message, we'll get back to you pronto. *Gracias!*"

She's not home, either. Elizabeth's frown deepened. *Maybe she's playing hooky. Or maybe . . .*

Just last night Jessica had told Elizabeth that she'd been sneaking off to the beach before school to practice surfing. A sequence of horrible pictures flashed through Elizabeth's mind. Jessica hauling Steven's bulky old surfboard to a deserted beach; Jessica trying to ride a huge wave but getting swamped; Jessica's helpless, broken body tumbling in the killer surf. *What if she had an accident?* thought Elizabeth, her pulse racing fearfully. *What if she fell and got knocked out by her board or something?*

Just as she hung up the phone, Elizabeth spotted an athletic blond boy crossing the lobby. "Ken!" she called out, beckoning urgently.

Ken joined her. "What's up, Liz?"

"It's Jessica," she said somewhat breathlessly.

"I meant to ask you," he said. "Is she sick?"

Elizabeth shook her head. "No, but I think she may be in trouble." Quickly, she told him about Jessica's secret early-morning outings.

Ken's jaw dropped. "She's been teaching herself to surf? Wow, I had no idea!"

"Me, either," said Elizabeth. "I think it's great, but I told her I also thought it was a little dangerous to go by herself, and today she didn't show up at school and she's not at home and I'm really worried that she might have had an accident so I think we should—"

Ken finished the sentence for her. "Go to the beach and look for her. Come on." He jingled his car keys. "I'll drive!"

Together they raced out to the student parking lot. Jessica's life could be on the line—there wasn't a minute to lose.

Jessica was pretty sure she'd died and gone to heaven. The midday sun was warm on her body, a fresh sea breeze caressed her skin . . . and Christian's strong arms were locked around her in an embrace she hoped would last forever.

They'd been kissing nonstop for about an hour. Now Jessica nestled in the crook of Christian's arm with her head on his shoulder. "I'm so happy I could burst," she said with a contented sigh.

Christian stroked her hair. "Let's play hooky for the rest of our lives, stay right here on this spot forever."

"Fine with me," said Jessica. "I don't ever want to go back to Sweet Valley High."

As soon as she and Christian had spotted each other in the misty dawn, their resolution to stay apart had crumbled like a sand castle before the rising tide. It felt so good to be together again, they'd ditched school to surf all morning, then collapsed in a deliciously tired tangle of limbs on the beach blanket.

Jessica propped herself up on one elbow. "Sweet Valley High," she repeated. She traced her index finger on Christian's sun-bronzed chest, smiling. "I'm one of the enemy. You're sure you don't hate me?"

"I wasn't happy hearing about the quarterback boyfriend part," Christian admitted. "But I could never hate you, Jessica." He pulled her to him again. "I love you."

Their lips met in a sweet, lingering kiss that left Jessica breathless. "I love you, too," she whispered. "But it's funny, isn't it?" She nibbled his earlobe. "We still don't really know anything about each other. Like, how come I didn't figure out you went to Palisades? Do you play sports? Since I'm a cheerleader, I'm at practically all the games."

"Basketball," said Christian.

She shook her head. "I don't remember you. How can I not remember you?"

He wound a strand of her hair around his finger, laughing. "If it's any consolation, I don't remember you, either, and I usually make a point of checking out the cheerleaders."

"What else?" asked Jessica. Suddenly, after weeks of mystery, she was hungry to know everything there was to know about Christian Gorman. "Tell me about your family."

"Mom's a doctor, Dad works for a brokerage firm. They're both workaholics—we never see them."

"We?"

"I told you about my older brother, Jason, once, remember? And I have a sister, Celia. She's in junior high. What about you?"

"I'm the baby of the family. My big brother, Steven, goes to Sweet Valley University," Jessica told him. "And Elizabeth's just a few minutes older than me. If you play basketball, you probably know her boyfriend, Todd Wilkins."

"Right. High scorer for your team last season. We still beat you, though."

Jessica's happy smile faded. "How did we get back on the subject of school rivalry?"

"I don't know." Christian sighed heavily. "Maybe because no matter how much we wish we were the only two people on the planet, that we could hide out at the beach forever, it's always going to be there."

"Always is a long time." Jessica's chin trembled. "*Too* long."

Christian touched the back of his hand gently to her cheek. "I agree. And you know what?" He sat up on the blanket, a hard, clear light shining in his eyes. "I'm going to put a stop to this thing. For you. For us."

"But how?"

"The guys trust me and look up to me." His expression was rueful. "I mean, I'm one of the people who started this whole mess. The time we decorated the Sweet Valley guys' yards with toilet paper and egged their cars? That was my idea, I'm not proud to say. So now I'll tell them the war's gone on long enough, that I've decided it's dumb."

Jessica smiled through her tears, her heart soaring with newfound hope. "Do you really think you can do it?"

"I can try." He put his arms around her and clasped her to him tightly. "There's a football game tonight, against Fort Carroll. I'll talk to everyone afterward."

"And if they don't listen?"

"They'll have to. That's all."

Christian spoke with such confidence, such strength and certainty, that immediately Jessica felt as if an enormous weight had been lifted from her shoulders. *An end to the war between Sweet Valley High and Palisades High!* she thought joyfully. *Tomorrow it'll be all over. And that means . . .*

What? Jessica recalled Christian's words. *We can't hide out on the beach forever,* she reminded herself. *We're not the only two people on the planet.* An end to the war wasn't going to solve all her problems. She'd still have to make a painful choice. What was she going to do about Ken?

Chapter 6

Bruce closed the door, then hitched himself up on the teacher's desk at the front of the classroom. "We're all here except Matthews," he observed briskly, scanning the group lounging in the desks facing him. "Anybody seen him?"

Winston checked the clock over the door. Lunch period was already half over. "I think we should go ahead without him," he proposed, "before we get booted out of here." *And maybe kicked out of school, too,* he added to himself.

In defiance of the new school rules, most of the guys sported Sweet Valley High baseball caps they'd pulled out of their back pockets as soon as they were safely out of view of any teachers or administrators prowling the corridors. Todd took off his plain black hooded sweatshirt, revealing an

"SVH Basketball" T-shirt underneath. Aaron wore one red sock and one white one. *Are we rebels,* Winston wondered, adjusting the brim of his own cap, *or just idiots?*

"OK." Bruce pounded on the desk for attention. "I've been thinking about a way to get back at Palisades, and I came up with a plan. They've got a big football game tonight."

"Against Fort Carroll, right?" said Ronnie.

"Yep," Bruce confirmed. "Now, my idea is we sneak over there ourselves, only we don't go to the game, we just go to the parking lot." He paused dramatically, taking something from his pocket. There was a gleam of silver as Bruce flipped open the blade on his Swiss army knife. "And slash the tires on the cars of certain individuals, whom I'm sure we all agree deserve that and worse."

There was a moment of surprised silence. Winston was the first to react. "Whoa, Patman," he said, rising to his feet. "I think that's a little extreme. A prank is one thing, like what they did to us with the toilet paper and eggs. But slashing tires . . ." He met Todd's eyes and saw a flash of agreement. "That's vandalism. Plain illegal. Not for me, buddy."

Bruce glared at Winston. "Are you saying we should let them get away with humiliating us?"

"No, man," Winston assured Bruce. "But how about just letting the air out of their tires?"

Bruce tightened his jaw. "That doesn't go far enough," he stated, his voice ice-cold. "I'm slashing some tires tonight. Who's with me and who isn't?"

Winston glanced again at Todd, hoping he'd speak up and help reason with Bruce, but this time Todd avoided Winston's gaze. *If Wilkins won't take my side, then no one will,* Winston realized.

He was right. One by one, the guys declared, "With you, Patman."

"All the way," Ronnie added.

Only Winston, still standing, was silent. "Looks like you're outvoted, Egbert," Bruce sneered. "So what'll it be?"

Winston shifted his weight from one foot to the other. *I could tell the principal,* he thought. *No names, just an anonymous tip. Then Palisades could arrange to have extra security at the game—stop this before it gets started.* "I—," Winston began.

"If anyone squeals . . ." Bruce cut in, his tone ominous.

Winston gulped, hoping his face wasn't turning red. *Did he read my mind?* he wondered.

"I'll blame you personally, Egbert," Bruce finished. "You'll be Sweet Valley High public enemy numero uno."

"Hey." Winston lifted his hands in mock surrender. "I was just going to say I'm with you, too."

"You'd better be," said Bruce, "because there's lots

of work to do, and we'll need all hands. So let's meet at the Dairi Burger at seven. Wear dark clothing and don't forget to bring a knife with a good heavy blade. And while we're at it, what do you think about tagging the Palisades cars with red and white spray paint?"

Todd and Aaron talked Bruce out of that one, but the tire-slashing plan stayed fixed. The bell rang and the boys loped quickly to the door, covering up their illicit T-shirts and pocketing their baseball caps as they went. "The Dairi Burger. Seven sharp," Bruce hissed as they emerged into the crowded hallway.

Winston gave Bruce a brisk nod and flashed a conspiratorial smile at Todd and the others. Inside, though, a nervous, slightly sick feeling rumbled in his stomach. He'd be at the Dairi Burger that night and he'd go to Palisades and he'd slash tires if that was what it took to prove his loyalty to Sweet Valley High. He'd stand by his buddies—he'd play his part. *But I don't have to like it,* Winston thought, melting into the river of students, his shoulders slumping. *I'm just not cut out for this cloak-and-dagger stuff!*

"You think she's at one of the town beaches?" Ken asked Elizabeth as he raced the Toyota toward the coast.

"I have no idea," Elizabeth admitted. "Don't surfers hang out at Ocean Bay?"

"Yeah, but the waves are better at Moon Beach and Jackson's Bluff. You're sure she didn't say where?"

"No," Elizabeth said. "I guess we'll just have to drive by all the town beaches."

The traffic signal ahead of them switched from green to yellow. Ken stepped on the gas and made it through the intersection before the light turned red. A few minutes later they were heading up the coast highway, their eyes peeled for a black Jeep parked in any of the duneside lots. "Here, call home one more time," Ken instructed Elizabeth, handing her his new cellular phone. "Maybe she's there now."

Elizabeth dialed the number. After a pause she shook her head. "I got the machine again."

Ken's fingers tightened on the steering wheel. Ghastly scenarios played themselves out in his imagination: Jessica knocked out by her surfboard, dragged out to sea by a treacherous undertow, stricken with a cramp. It was easy to have an accident, and she'd been so distracted lately. Ever since the night of the dance, of the fight . . .

And I've been a macho jerk, Ken thought. He was totally focused on the war with Palisades—he'd let it become the most important thing in his life. At that very moment he was supposed to be at another one of Bruce's stupid strategy meetings. *I didn't even know about this surfing thing,* he accused himself. *I've been ignoring her.* "If anything happens to her, I'll never forgive myself," he muttered out loud.

Elizabeth placed a hand on his arm. "She'll be OK. She *has* to be OK."

Ken wanted to believe Elizabeth. But as they sped past the beach parking lots one by one and didn't see the Jeep in any of them, his worry increased. What if they didn't find her?

"There's only one more little beach up this way," Ken said to Elizabeth. "If she's not there, I vote we drive down to Moon Beach and—"

"She's there!" Elizabeth cried, pointing. "I see the Jeep!"

Ken slammed on the brakes and dragged hard on the wheel, steering the Toyota into the parking lot. Sure enough, there was the twins' black Jeep. The only other vehicle in the lot was a powder blue VW van.

Elizabeth was out of the car before Ken even killed the engine. Pocketing his keys, he sprinted after her past the sign posted on the dune warning of dangerous tides and undertows. "Do you see her?" he called, putting a hand to his forehead to shield his eyes from the blinding noon sun.

"No, but the surfboard's not in the Jeep. She must be out there somewhere." Elizabeth stood at the water's edge, scanning the waves frantically.

In tense, fearful silence they both studied the ocean. The surf was up. Perfect wave after perfect wave rolled toward shore, but Jessica wasn't riding any of them. *She's out there, though,* thought Ken, crazy with worry. *I've got to get to her before . . . if it isn't already too late. . . .* He tore off his shirt, then kicked aside his sneakers.

"What are you doing?" cried Elizabeth.

Ken was already wading into the foaming surf. The water hit his knees, his waist. A wave was about to crash onto him. He dived under it.

When he broke the surface and started swimming, he could hear Elizabeth shouting, her voice faint in the wind. "There's a bad undertow here, Ken! Come back!"

Ken didn't heed her plea. Only one thing mattered right now: reaching Jessica, saving Jessica. Summoning all his strength, he stroked powerfully through the huge waves.

"I feel like I'm drowning," Jessica whispered to Christian.

"Me, too," he whispered back.

They were lost in a fog of breathless kisses. At some point Christian had offered to jog down to the next beach to pick up lunch at the snack bar, but somehow in the middle of discussing what kind of sandwiches and sodas to buy, they'd started kissing again. Once they got their hands on each other, they couldn't seem to stop.

Jessica had kissed plenty of boys, and she'd been in love before, seriously in love—but she'd never felt quite like this. *It's like we've always known each other somehow, and at the same time it's so exciting and brand-new,* she thought, gazing deep into Christian's soulful blue eyes. *Like we're meant to be together. He's my destiny.* Jessica knew that fate had brought them to the same place at the same time that first morning on the beach. Things just had to work out, it was that simple. The high school war would end, and Sweet Valley and Palisades kids would forget that they'd hated each other. Jessica would break up with Ken and eventually start dating Christian openly, and no one would care.

The sound of distant shouting penetrated Jessica's reverie. "What's that?" she murmured, her mouth still close to Christian's.

"Someone's crashing our party," he answered, "and they're making a lot of noise."

Jessica sat up. Sure enough, they no longer had the beach to themselves. A blond girl in jeans and a bright purple T-shirt was waving her arms and running in their direction. "Oh, no," gasped Jessica, clapping a hand to her mouth. "It's Liz!"

She and Christian both jumped to their feet. "Liz?" he asked.

"My twin sister. But what on earth is she *doing* here?" Elizabeth drew closer, visibly distraught. *Something's wrong. Really wrong,* thought Jessica, her mouth going dry. *Liz wouldn't have tracked me down unless* . . . "Maybe they found out somehow. K-k-ken and the guys," Jessica stuttered. "Maybe they're coming after us. After *you*."

She clung to Christian's arm, picturing him beaten up mercilessly by a vengeful Sweet Valley mob led by her own boyfriend. *And what would they do to me?* she wondered.

As Elizabeth approached, a panicked squeak escaped Jessica's throat. "Liz, what—"

Elizabeth threw her arms around her sister. "Jess, you're all right!" she cried, gasping for breath. "We were so worried. We thought you'd drowned, that you'd had an accident surfing, and Ken's swimming out to look for you, and *he* could drown and—" Elizabeth stopped. Still panting, she focused on Christian for the first time, her eyebrows furrowed with suspicion. "Jess?" she said, a questioning note in her voice.

Christian's arm was wrapped around Jessica's shoulders, and she was pressing her body close to his side. *We look guilty,* Jessica realized. *Very guilty.*

Jessica turned, looking up into Christian's eyes. "You should get out of here," she said. "Before . . ." She shot a desperate glance down the beach.

Fortunately, Ken was nowhere in sight.

Christian cupped her face in his hands. "Are you sure? I'm not afraid to—"

"I know you're not, but it's better if you and he don't . . . after tonight things will be different," she whispered. "But for now . . ."

"OK." Christian bent his head, brushing her lips with a kiss. "I'll see you."

Lifting his surfboard under one arm, Christian disappeared behind a dune covered with tall waving beach grass. At that very same instant Ken waded out of the water fifty yards down the beach and, spotting them, began to jog in their direction.

Elizabeth put her hands on her hips. "Jessica, what on earth is going on?"

"Please, Liz. Don't tell Ken," Jessica begged.

"But who was that?"

"Don't say anything to Ken," Jessica repeated, her eyes wild. "Don't say anything to anyone. Promise me, Liz!"

Elizabeth hesitated for an agonizing moment. Then, to Jessica's profound relief, she nodded reluctantly. "I promise, but later you'd better explain—"

Elizabeth didn't finish her sentence. Ken was in earshot. Jessica drew a deep breath, composing the features of her face into innocent lines, willing her heart to stop hammering. *Get ready to tell some more lies,* she told herself dismally. The strain was bound to start showing soon. How long could she keep this up?

Elizabeth drove the Jeep back to school, and Jessica rode with Ken in his Toyota. "Playing hooky to surf? All by yourself? I don't get it. What's going on with you?" he asked, steering with one hand and rubbing her knee with the other.

"I don't know." Jessica tried to sound nonchalant even though she was still rattled by the close call on the beach. Five more seconds and Ken and Christian would have been face-to-face . . . with her in the middle. "I just needed a day off, I guess."

"You should have told me," he chided her. "I would've cut classes, too."

"It was more like . . . I wanted to be alone."

Ken cocked his eyebrows, looking a little offended. "Alone?"

Jessica stroked his arm with as much affection as she could muster. "Nothing personal. Sometimes it just feels good to go off by yourself, you know?"

"What about this surfing thing?" Ken prodded. "How'd that start?"

At this question Jessica went completely blank. "Oh, well, I . . ." For a split second she didn't have the foggiest recollection of what had originally sent her into the water with her board. Surfing had become forever connected to being with Christian. *The competition!* she remembered with a rush of relief. *Rock TV. Lila. The bet!*

She told Ken the whole story . . . up to a point. He still appeared mystified. "Yeah, but why keep it a secret?" he wondered. "I'm worried about you, Jess. You're just not yourself these days."

I'm not, she agreed silently. *If you only knew!*

They were parked now in the student lot at Sweet Valley High. Ken slipped off his seat belt and turned to face Jessica. "You're still upset about what happened the other night," he guessed. "The fight. The whole war with Palisades."

He'd hit the nail on the head. Jessica didn't have to lie this time. "It really shook me up," she admitted.

She grasped the door handle, but before she could step from the car, Ken leaned over to hug her protectively. "I'll always take care of you. You know that, don't you, Jess?" he murmured into her hair.

Jessica nodded. "Yeah."

"So stop worrying. After tonight . . ."

"Tonight?" Jessica thought about Christian's plan to talk to his Palisades buddies after the Fort Carroll football game. "What *about* tonight?"

"I think things are going to be all right," Ken said, not answering her question directly. "I wish we could be together tonight, but actually I have someplace else to be. A GNO."

When Ken, Bruce, and the rest of the gang had first instituted "Guys' Night Out," Jessica had thought it was ridiculous. Now she welcomed the diversion. "I understand," she said.

"I just hate being away from you," he said, rubbing his cheek against hers, then kissing her softly on the lips. "We don't get to do enough of this."

Jessica nodded, meanwhile letting out a secret sigh of relief. GNOs were looking better and better to her all the time. Any excuse to avoid intimacy with Ken. Because the less time they spent together, the less likely she'd slip up and give away the fact that her heart now belonged to Christian.

Chapter 7

"I don't know how useful that was," Penny said in a low voice to Elizabeth as the first joint Sweet Valley High–Palisades High task-force meeting broke up. "I mean, obviously everybody on the committee really wants a better relationship between the two schools. But it's kind of like preaching to the converted. The people whose attitudes need changing are going to be the hardest to reach."

Elizabeth nodded. "Penny, before we leave, can you wait a second? I want to talk to Caitlin."

"Sure," agreed Penny. "I'm not in a hurry."

Elizabeth went back into the conference room where the meeting had been held. The Palisades High students and teachers were saying their good-byes. Only Caitlin stood apart, bending over her book bag.

"Caitlin," said Elizabeth, putting a hand on her friend's arm. "Are you all right?"

When Caitlin looked up, Elizabeth could see that her dark eyes were red-rimmed, as if she'd been crying. And she'd seemed on the verge of tears all through the meeting. "Do you want to go someplace and talk?" Elizabeth asked gently.

In response Caitlin grasped Elizabeth by the arm and led her to the far end of the conference room, where a door opened into a palm-filled courtyard. As soon as they were outside, Caitlin buried her face in her hands and burst into tears.

"Oh, Liz," she sobbed.

Elizabeth slipped a comforting arm around Caitlin's shoulders. "What's the matter?"

"It's—it's Doug," Caitlin stammered. "We—we . . . last night. We broke up."

"Oh, no," Elizabeth exclaimed. "But, Caitlin, you two have been going out for years! What happened?"

"This," said Caitlin bitterly as she gestured back toward the conference room. "The high school war. We've been arguing about it so much, you know? He's totally into the rivalry, and I think we should try to be friends with you guys."

Elizabeth nodded. She knew only too well.

"When he found out I'd joined the task force, he went ballistic." Caitlin sniffled. "He said if I couldn't back him up, then obviously I didn't really love him. So I said if he wasn't willing to let me make up my own mind about things, then *he* didn't really love *me*. And that was that."

"It'll blow over," Elizabeth predicted. "You'll get back together when things calm down a little."

"I don't think so." Caitlin dug a packet of tissues out of her black leather shoulder bag and blew her nose. "He's already hanging out with Britta Jantzen, this disgustingly cute sophomore who just flutters her eyelashes at him and tells him that he's big and strong and tough for standing up to Sweet Valley. No, it's over for good."

Elizabeth gave Caitlin a squeeze, but she couldn't think of anything else to say that would make her friend feel better. "I'm sorry, Caitlin."

"Me, too." A single tear rolled down Caitlin's olive-skinned cheek. "But I guess I shouldn't be surprised. I mean, how could we go on loving each other if we can't see eye to eye on something this important?"

Elizabeth didn't answer the question. She was afraid, too, because she wasn't thinking about Caitlin and Doug anymore—she was thinking about herself and Todd. *We don't see eye to eye these days, either,* Elizabeth reflected, her heart contracting painfully. *Does that mean we're doomed to break up, too?*

* * *

An hour after the task-force meeting, Elizabeth stood at the kitchen counter at home, chopping onions and carrots to throw in with the beef stew she was making for dinner. When she heard a car in the driveway, she looked out the window over the sink in time to see Jessica hop out of Lila's green Triumph.

Elizabeth met her sister in the front hallway. "Did you go to cheerleading practice?" she asked conversationally.

Jessica nodded. Sidestepping, she tried to get past Elizabeth. "Excuse me."

Elizabeth continued to block her path. "Not until you tell me about the guy at the beach."

At that moment the phone rang. Automatically, Elizabeth moved to answer it. Seizing her opportunity, Jessica dodged past her sister and galloped up the stairs.

After scribbling down a message for her mother, who was still at the office of her interior-design firm, Elizabeth ran upstairs after her twin. Jessica's door was shut. Elizabeth jiggled the knob and discovered that the door was locked, too. "Open up, Jess," Elizabeth shouted over the sound of Jessica's stereo.

"I'm busy," came Jessica's muffled reply.

"No, you're not. Let me in!"

A full minute passed. Finally the door eased open a crack and Jessica peered out. "What do you want?"

Elizabeth pushed into the room. Crossing to the stereo, she turned down the volume, then perched on the edge of Jessica's bed, her arms folded across her chest. "I'm not budging until you spill the beans," she informed her sister. "Who's the hunk?"

She expected a flip answer. It wasn't the first time Jessica had been juggling two—or more—boys at once, and it wasn't the first time her twin sister had caught her in the act, either. But Jessica didn't even crack a smile. Her face pale, she pressed her lips tightly together, maintaining an obstinate silence.

"Come on," Elizabeth pressed. "I'm doing you a *huge* favor—I promised I wouldn't tell Ken. So you owe me. What's his name? Where's he from? How'd you meet him? And how long has this been going on?"

To her surprise, Jessica's eyes filled with tears. "I can't tell you, Liz," Jessica whispered.

"Why? I really do swear I won't tell Ken, if that's what you're worried about. I won't tell Todd. I won't tell anyone."

"It's not that." Jessica dashed the tears from her face with the back of her hand. "Liz, I just can't—please don't—" Jessica stopped, shaking her head to indicate that she couldn't go on.

Elizabeth stared at her sister for a long, silent moment. When the phone on Jessica's nightstand rang, they both jumped.

Jessica answered it. "It's for you," she said, making a point of not offering the receiver to her sister. "Todd."

"I'll get it in my room," said Elizabeth.

Cutting through the bathroom to her own room, Elizabeth heard Jessica lock the door behind her. She considered turning around, knocking, trying one more time to find out what was going on with her sister. Instead, she picked up the phone. "Hi, Todd," she said. "What's up? When do you want to come over?"

"That's why I'm calling," he answered. "I have to break our study date. Hope that's OK."

Elizabeth sat down in her desk chair, twining the phone cord around her index finger. "No problem. I can get someone else to quiz me for the history test. Something came up?"

"Actually . . ." Todd cleared his throat in an embarrassed fashion. "It turns out there's a GNO tonight."

"A Guys' Night Out?" Elizabeth asked, suspicious. "On a school night?"

"Don't worry, we won't go looking for trouble," Todd assured her, too quickly, Elizabeth thought.

"Aaron said something about going bowling, getting pizza."

"What about the history test?"

"Oh, I feel pretty on top of the material. I'll see you in school tomorrow."

"Right," Elizabeth said coolly.

"I love you, Liz."

She hesitated before repeating the words. "I love you, too, Todd."

After hanging up the phone, though, she wished she'd stayed on the line longer in order to express her true feelings. "A GNO," she fumed under her breath. "Like I don't know what that *really* means. Bowling—yeah, right." It was obvious Todd and the gang were getting together in order to plot mischief against Palisades. *Or maybe they're past the plotting stage,* Elizabeth worried, looking out her window at the sinking sun. *What if they go after those guys? What if there's another fight?*

Panic welled up inside her as she realized how much emotional distance there was between her and Todd at that moment. *We're leading separate lives,* she thought. Suspicion and estrangement had taken the place of sympathy and companionship. *This is probably how it started for Caitlin and Doug. . . .*

And then there was Jessica's stubborn silence about the mystery man from the beach. Something was wrong, Elizabeth deduced, and it wasn't just that Jessica was bummed about being caught by her sister running around behind her boyfriend's back. In the old days Jessica would have laughed off something like that. At the very least she would have relaxed once she felt sure Elizabeth wouldn't rat on her. But when Elizabeth had pressed her on the subject, she'd seen something she didn't expect in Jessica's eyes.

Fear.

Elizabeth sat in baffled, anxious silence, staring out the window at the sky, now plum-colored with dusk. In one sense she knew precisely where she was: at her desk, in her room, in her family's house on Calico Drive. But in another sense she felt totally at sea—lost and confused.

A lot of things seemed to be going on—dangerous things. Things she didn't understand and couldn't control. And she didn't like any of it.

At five minutes past seven, Ken parked his car in the parking lot of the Dairi Burger, a popular hangout for Sweet Valley teens. Dressed in denim jackets and dark sunglasses, Bruce, Todd, Winston, and a bunch of the other guys were already at a big table in the back near the jukebox.

Ken considered swinging by the take-out counter to buy a milk shake, but he could see Bruce drumming his fingers impatiently on the table. *Time to get down to business,* Ken reminded himself. *This isn't really a GNO—we're not here to socialize.*

He dropped onto a chair, straddling it backward. "Evening," he drawled in his best western-cowpoke imitation, pretending to push an invisible Stetson back from his forehead.

Winston grinned, but Bruce's expression remained intensely serious. "OK, we're all here," Bruce said, planting his elbows on the table. "Before we get started, I want to make sure of something, though." His eyes raked their faces, one by one. "I want to be sure that when we get to Palisades, nobody's going to wimp out. Because if one of us messes up, the rest of us will get nailed."

When Bruce's eyes settled on Ken's face, Ken didn't blink. But he noticed that a couple of the guys shifted uncomfortably in their seats. Winston, especially, looked as if he had a whole colony of ants in his pants.

Ken decided it couldn't hurt to express the reservations some of the others seemed to be feeling. "I missed the powwow at lunch," he remarked, "but I assume you took a vote"—he lowered his voice—"on this tire-slashing deal. Was it unanimous? Everyone's for it one hundred percent?"

Todd shrugged. Aaron ran a hand through his

hair, staying quiet. Winston continued to squirm, but he didn't comment.

Ronnie spoke up. "Yeah, it was unanimous," he declared brashly. "You saying you don't think it's a good idea, Matthews?"

If the rest of the gang was up for it, Ken wasn't about to sit home. "No, just checking."

"Good." Bruce unfolded a small piece of paper. "I spent the afternoon figuring out which cars to hit. I'm going to make assignments—everybody gets a car. First there's McMullen's green Range Rover. Who wants that one?"

Ken could feel the knife in the back pocket of his jeans. Suddenly he was itching to use it—he hadn't forgotten the Palisades linebacker's insults after the last football game, or the pain of McMullen's fist punching his stomach. "Give him to me," he growled.

Bruce ticked off the rest of the targeted cars. "We've got a red Mustang convertible, vanity plates 'HOT ROD.' A white Corolla, a green Saab, a red Chevy Blazer with silver stripes, a black Honda Prelude, a white BMW, a blue Taurus wagon."

"Somebody's mom's car," remarked Aaron. "Man, is she going to be bummed!"

Bruce chuckled maliciously. "And last but not least, Gorman's light blue VW van."

Ken's ears pricked up at this. "Wait a minute,"

he said. "I just saw one of those someplace."

Bruce and the rest of the guys were already on their feet heading toward the exit. As Ken followed, he remembered where he'd seen the powder blue van. *The beach today. It was parked near Jessica's Jeep when Liz and I got there, but it was gone when we left.*

The coincidence struck Ken as more than a little strange. Did it mean anything, though? "Hey, Wilkins, what do you think about the fact that—" he started to ask as they pushed out the door into the Dairi Burger parking lot.

But Bruce was shouting out more orders. "Let's just take a couple of cars. You can ride with me, Matthews." Bruce pointed a stern finger at Winston. "You, too, Egbert. I want to keep an eye on you."

Ken pocketed his own car keys and squeezed into the cramped backseat of the black Porsche with license plates "1BRUCE1." As Bruce revved the powerful engine, Ken felt the adrenaline flood his veins. His muscles coiled taut with energy, ready to explode into action.

The puzzle of the light blue VW van nagged at him momentarily, but he pushed the thought aside. It was time to go to Palisades.

Elizabeth planted her heel on the living-room carpet and pivoted. "When Todd told me there was another GNO tonight, I just knew it meant trouble," she said to Enid, Marla, and Caitlin, who were sitting in a row on the couch.

"The guys only get together these days for one reason," agreed Enid as she tore open a bag of pretzels and poured them into a bowl.

Marla reached for a pretzel. "You don't think they're planning to start a fight after our football game against Fort Carroll tonight, do you?"

"I have no idea," said Elizabeth, continuing to pace nervously. "Todd acted totally innocent. I didn't get a crumb of honest information from him. But I think we have to assume the worst, which is why I called you. We can't wait for the task force to take action—we need to do something now!"

The doorbell rang and she hurried to answer it. DeeDee, Penny, and Maria entered, just as Jessica drifted downstairs. At the sight of Maria's red-and-white SVH cheerleading jacket, Jessica shook her finger playfully. "School colors. Tsk, tsk."

Maria grimaced. "I completely forgot—I just grabbed the first thing in the closet. Chrome Dome's not coming to the meeting, though, is he?"

Elizabeth ushered the newcomers into the living room to join the others. "So who has an idea?" she asked, eager to get started. "What's the best way to keep Sweet Valley and Palisades guys apart?"

To her surprise, her twin sister was the first to

speak up. "You shouldn't worry so much, Liz," said Jessica. "I have a hunch that after tonight, the war will be history."

Elizabeth couldn't disguise her skepticism. "What—do you think there's going to be some kind of divine intervention?"

Jessica smiled enigmatically. "I just think the guys are going to see the light, that's all."

Maria shook her head. "I'm afraid not, Jess. The war isn't going away. Liz is right. The GNO is just a cover."

"How do you know?" asked Caitlin.

"Because when Winston gave me the GNO story, I hounded him until he told the truth. I think he wanted me to know—I could tell he felt awful about it. You won't believe what they're planning to do!"

The rest of the girls leaned forward in their seats. "What?" Elizabeth asked.

"They're going to Palisades tonight, and while all the Palisades students are at the football game . . . I really can't believe they're doing this," Maria exclaimed. "I can't believe Winston would be dumb enough to go along with it. Just because Bruce and the rest of the gang are so out-of-control macho!"

"What? What?" prodded Elizabeth, bursting with curiosity.

"Supposedly Bruce made a list of what kinds of

cars the Palisades High guys drive, and the Sweet Valley guys are going to slash their tires."

"Slash their tires?" Elizabeth repeated, gaping at Maria. Marla and Caitlin also stared, their faces white with shock.

Maria nodded. "I told you it was bad!"

It *was* bad, far worse even than Elizabeth had imagined. *And Todd's mixed up in it,* she thought, her stomach twisting in a sickening knot. *He's off slashing tires like some juvenile delinquent.*

On the other side of the room, Jessica had just taken a pretzel from the bowl. Now her fingers clasped convulsively, snapping the pretzel in two. Elizabeth shot a look at her sister. *Are you still so sure the animosity's about to end?* she wanted to ask, but didn't. The answer was written clearly on Jessica's pale, stricken face.

"What are we going to do?" wondered Enid, her green eyes clouded with distress. "Is it too late to drive over there and try to stop them?"

Elizabeth glanced at her watch. It was almost nine o'clock. "The football game will be over soon, but if we—"

"I can't believe you let this happen!" Caitlin burst out, her eyes flashing with anger. "I can't believe you Sweet Valley girls knew about this and didn't try to stop it!"

"You say you want peace," agreed Marla, tossing

her curly auburn hair, "but you're as much to blame for the war as the boys!"

The Palisades girls jumped to their feet and started to storm out the door. Elizabeth ran to intercept them. "Wait," she begged, placing a hand on Caitlin's arm. "Please don't leave. We want peace as much as you do. You know that!"

Caitlin and Marla exchanged an intense, wordless glance. "We have to stick together, now more than ever," Elizabeth continued earnestly. "We need your help. We can't do it without you."

Elizabeth held her breath. Finally Caitlin mustered an apologetic smile. "I've been kind of upset lately, as you know. I really saw red for a minute there. But I shouldn't be mad at you, Liz."

"I'm sorry, too," said Marla. "I didn't mean what I said. You all aren't to blame—you're not the ones off slashing tires."

Off slashing tires . . . Elizabeth repeated to herself. Her relief at holding on to her Palisades allies mingled with her own sense of outrage. She pictured Todd and the other guys sneaking around the Palisades parking lot, switchblades in hand. Were they wearing stockings over their heads? Ski masks? Todd, the star basketball player; Ken, the football captain; Winston, the best-liked student in the junior class. "They're supposed to be leaders and role models," said Elizabeth in disgust. "What a cowardly, rotten thing to do!"

She began fumbling in the hall closet for a jacket. "Where are you going, Liz?" Enid called.

"To Palisades," Elizabeth declared. "To stop them. To stop the vandalism."

Now it was Caitlin's turn to place a restraining hand on Elizabeth's arm. "I wish we could stop them, but at this point I think we'd better stay out of it."

"If the guys are worked up into one of their idiotic macho frenzies, having their girlfriends show up would only make things worse," DeeDee concurred.

Elizabeth sank into an armchair, limp with defeat. "So what *can* we do?"

"I don't know," said Marla, "but one thing's for sure. If your guys really *do* slash our guys' tires, we're going to have a major situation on our hands."

"And a couple of measly editorials won't solve the problem," predicted Caitlin with a gloomy sigh.

Winston, Bruce, Ken, Todd, Aaron, Ron, Bill, and Zack huddled in a shadowy corner of the Palisades High School parking lot. "You know what to do," hissed Bruce, his voice tight with suppressed excitement. "The game'll let out any minute now, so there's no time to waste. Let's go!"

The boys fanned out, roaming the aisles of the parking lot. Winston loped at Todd's side, a flashlight in his hand so he could double-check the license plate of his intended victim's car. Spotting a white Corolla, he swung the beam of his flashlight over the car's rear plate. "Nope. Wrong car. What are we doing here, anyway?" he muttered.

Todd fingered his unopened Swiss army knife. "You got me," he admitted. "But having come this far, we can't exactly—"

At that instant they heard a cry of triumph from the other end of the parking lot. "Patman," said Winston. "He must've found the red Mustang."

A few more war whoops reached their ears. "We'd better get cracking. Look." Todd pointed to the football stands. A few people were starting to drift in the direction of the parking lot. "The game must be over!"

Todd sprinted off, knife in hand, leaving Winston standing flat-footed. *This is it,* Winston told himself. Any minute now Palisades and Fort Carroll students would pour into the lot. If he and his friends didn't act fast, they'd get caught red-handed. *And I can't be the only one who doesn't slash some tires,* thought Winston. *Bruce would never let me live it down.*

Time was running out, but still Winston felt paralyzed. He moved up and down the aisles slowly, as if he were walking through water, pushing some heavy weight with his body. When he finally located the car he had been assigned, he stared at it for a long, conscience-racked moment. *Do I really want to do this?* he asked himself. *Is this fair?*

An urgent shout broke through his indecision. "Hurry up, Egbert!"

Winston turned to see Todd waving at him from the other end of the parking lot. The rest of the guys were there, too, ready to make their getaway.

Do it, Winston commanded himself, *before those bruisers from Palisades show up and you get yourself scalped!*

He took the knife from his pocket and gripped the handle tightly. Out of the corner of his eye, he was aware of movement in the distance—people flooding from the stands into the parking lot. Taking a deep breath, Winston plunged the blade of the knife into one and then the other of the Corolla's rear tires.

Two out of four, he thought, panting. *That'll have to do. This guy won't be driving anyplace tonight, anyhow.* Spinning around, he catapulted forward as if he were running a hundred-yard dash.

But someone else was just as quick. Before he'd taken two strides, Winston felt a massive hand grip his shoulder, stopping him in his tracks. "Hey, what do you think you're doing?" a rough voice demanded.

Adrenaline shot through Winston's veins. In a

surge of strength, he twisted free from the other boy's grasp. His shirt ripped, but he didn't care. He was too busy running for his life.

He didn't look back, so he didn't see the boy's face, but he knew he'd never forget the voice. As Winston bolted, arms and legs pumping like crazy and his heart hammering in his throat, the boy shouted again, chilling words that Winston knew he'd be hearing in his dreams. "You're dead, man. You're *dead*!"

Chapter 8

The morning was misty and cool, with barely any wind, and no waves. Instead of surfing, Jessica and Christian cuddled on an inflatable mattress in the back of his VW bus.

"We shouldn't meet here anymore, now that Ken knows this is where I come to surf," said Jessica.

"You'll have to let me take you out on a real date, then," Christian replied. "How about this Saturday night?"

Jessica snuggled next to him under the blanket. "Sounds good. I didn't think you'd make it this morning, with your tires slashed and all."

"Two of the tires just got nicked—only one of them was really punctured. I patched it and pumped it back up. Somebody had a crummy knife," Christian said dryly.

"I'm so sorry," said Jessica, rubbing her hand in gentle circles on his bare chest. "I can't believe they did that to you. I mean, those guys are my friends." She wrinkled her forehead, confused. "At least they used to be."

Christian clenched his jaw. "Yeah, well, I'm sorry, too, and not just because of the damage to my VW. You know what this means, Jess."

She nodded miserably. "There's no way you'll be able to stop the war."

"I was going to talk to my buddies after the game last night," said Christian, "but when we got to the parking lot and saw all those cars with flat tires . . ." He whistled. "Man, you should have heard them. You should've heard *me*. I was steamed, too."

"So the war will go on and on." Jessica pressed herself close to Christian for comfort. "Palisades will get back at Sweet Valley, and then Sweet Valley will get back at Palisades, and the violence will get worse and worse. And where does that leave us?"

"I don't know, but I'm not planning to let you go." Christian's arms tightened around her. "No matter what happens."

"What about when your friends retaliate for the tire slashing?" Jessica imagined Christian with a knife, slashing tires. Or worse, fighting with Ken again. She shuddered. "You're their leader. They'll expect you to be first in line to get revenge against Sweet Valley."

"Well, I won't do it," declared Christian. "I'm through with the violence."

"But what will the other guys think?"

"I don't care what they think." Christian gazed into Jessica's eyes. "Don't you see? Falling in love with you has given me a new perspective on everything. The rivalry between our schools? It's meaningless. And if taking a stand means losing friends, then that's just the way it goes. You're more important," he said with quiet conviction.

Jessica nodded mutely, leaning her head against Christian's chest and listening to the strong, rhythmic beat of his heart. She felt the same way. She'd give up all her Sweet Valley friends for Christian if she had to. Would it come to that, though? Was it just a matter of time before her allegiance was put to the test? How was this all going to end?

Elizabeth and Todd stood near Elizabeth's locker before school on Wednesday morning, listening to Chrome Dome Cooper's announcement over the loudspeaker. The principal was asking for information about the vandalism at Palisades High School the previous night.

Frowning, Elizabeth slammed her locker door shut. "I really can't believe you guys did that," she said in a low, angry voice. "It was on the local news this morning, in the paper . . ."

"I know," said Todd with a half smile. "I haven't got such a big headline since I scored thirty points in the county championship game."

Elizabeth glared at him. "I can't believe you're proud of yourself!"

"I was just joking, Liz. I'm not proud." Todd's expression grew more serious. "But they deserved it, you know?"

She shook her head. "No, I *don't* know. I don't understand the rationale at all. But I can tell you one thing." Her eyes brimmed with tears. "I'd never tell the principal on you in a million years, but it really makes me sick. It's like you're a gang member or something. I'm just so disappointed, Todd. How can I love you and respect you if you act like this?"

"We didn't hurt anybody," Todd said in self-defense. "We did a little damage, but nothing that couldn't be fixed."

"But what about next time?" Elizabeth wiped her eyes on her sleeve. "Palisades won't take this lying down. What then?"

Todd shrugged, wedging his hands deep in the front pockets of his khakis. "We'll do what we have to do."

"Promise me you won't fight anymore,"

Elizabeth begged. "Promise you won't just go along with whatever sick thing Bruce tells you to do."

"I'm not just going along with Patman. I believe—"

"You believe what? You believe in vandalism and violence? Those are solutions?"

Todd was silent. Elizabeth pressed her point. "I love you, Todd, and I think you're a better person than that," she said softly, placing a hand on his arm. "I bet you could lead Bruce and the guys in a more positive direction. Talk them into calling a truce."

"That's what you want us to do? Wimp out? Wave the white flag? Let Palisades get the last laugh?"

"It wouldn't be wimping out. It's more like—"

"Wimping out," Todd cut in. "Elizabeth." He gripped her arms, looking hard into her face. "Can't you even try to understand? I'm doing this for you. I don't like it, but it's necessary."

Elizabeth stared up at her boyfriend. His tone was earnest, and she'd never seen his coffee brown eyes more sincere. She did what he asked—she tried to see his point of view. But it still didn't make any sense. *I'm supposed to be psyched that he's willing to shed blood for me?* she wondered, baffled. *I'm supposed to clap and cheer because he slashed some poor guy's tires? What planet does he come from?*

They'd been talking for hours, for days, about this issue, hashing it over and over, and they were no closer to reaching common ground. *We used to communicate so well,* Elizabeth thought bitterly, *and now it's like we speak two completely different languages.* As she remembered how Caitlin and Doug's relationship ended, Elizabeth felt perilously close to tears again. Todd just wasn't the same person she'd fallen in love with, and he'd probably say the same about her. Would they ever really understand each other again?

On his way to homeroom Ken stopped by Jessica's locker. She wasn't there, nor was she hanging out with Lila and Amy, or Elizabeth. *She must've gone surfing again,* Ken mused, doubling back to his own locker to grab his math book. It seemed weird. Why didn't she tell him about her plans, invite him along? What was going on with her?

"Morning, Matthews," said Bruce, falling into step beside Ken.

"Howdy, pardner," Ken replied.

Bruce grinned. "We scored big time last night, huh?"

"Front page," Ken agreed. "So watch your back, man. They're going to come after us."

"We can handle them," Bruce said with blustery confidence. "I'm not afraid of any Palisades punk."

He chuckled. "Besides, how will they come after us if all their cars are crippled?"

"We shouldn't get too cocky, or relax our guard," Ken said. "They'll definitely try to pull something. Maybe tonight, maybe tomorrow."

Bruce's eyes gleamed. "So perhaps a preemptive strike is in order. Let's think about this."

Ken noticed that a bunch of sophomore girls were listening to their conversation with interest. "Put a lid on it for now, though, would you, Patman?" Ken asked, lowering his voice. "I don't really want word to get around that it was us over at Palisades last night."

Bruce puffed out his chest. "You should be psyched, man. Anyway, you don't think everyone already knows?"

"Maybe they suspect," Ken conceded, "but that's different from its being official. I just don't want to end up in the principal's office—or in jail."

As they continued down the hall, though, Ken had to admit to himself that, like Bruce, he was kind of pumped, remembering the rush he'd got the night before when his knife had ripped through the tires of Greg McMullen's Range Rover. He didn't really mind if kids at school, particularly cute sophomore girls, thought he was partly responsible for the coup against Palisades. He could definitely live with the glory. *We're on top now, and that's bet-*

ter than being humiliated, he decided, *on or off the football field.* Then Ken grimaced. *As long as I don't get busted,* he amended silently.

"Like I was saying, preemptive strike." Bruce didn't bother whispering. "We need more dirt on these guys, though. Up for some intelligence gathering, Matthews?"

"You bet," said Ken, moving out of the flow of traffic and bending over to retie the lace on his left sneaker.

"How about you dig up some copies of the Palisades High newspaper, maybe a couple of recent yearbooks? I bet they have stuff like that in the *Oracle* office."

"Sure, but what for?"

"Knowledge," explained Bruce, a cold glint in his eye. "If we can figure out which clubs the Palisades guys are in, who they go out with, that kind of stuff, we'll be in a better position to hit them where it hurts."

For a split second Ken was ready to tell Bruce to forget it. Hit them where it hurts? He imagined the Palisades guys doing the same kind of research, finding out that he dated Jessica, maybe doing something to scare her. It seemed kind of low, going after people's girlfriends. Definitely unsportsmanlike.

Wait a minute, he reminded himself. Hadn't one

of the Palisades crew already scared Jessica half out of her wits, threatening her the night of the dance? Slashing tires was fine, but it hadn't *really* evened the score. "I'll do it," Ken agreed, his own eyes shining with a hard, determined light.

At the start of her free period Elizabeth waylaid Jessica in the Sweet Valley High girls' room. "Come on, I need to talk to you," she told her sister, dragging her down the hall to the newspaper office.

Inside, Elizabeth shut and locked the door. They had the office to themselves, so she felt free to really let Jessica have it. "You'll really end up in trouble if you keep missing homeroom, Jess," she lectured. "One more lateness and you get a week of detention."

Jessica shrugged, turning her head to avoid her sister's gaze. "So?"

"So it's stupid," said Elizabeth. She gripped Jessica's arm, giving her a little shake. "Look at me, Jess. Were you at the beach again this morning?"

Jessica shrugged once more. "What if I was?"

"With that guy?"

Jessica pressed her lips tightly together, but her silence told Elizabeth what she wanted to know. "You were with him. What's the story, Jess? Who is he? How long have you been seeing him? Is it serious?"

She expected Jessica to tell her to bug off and mind her own business. She *didn't* expect the tears that suddenly streamed down her twin's cheeks. "I can't tell you anything about him," Jessica choked out.

Elizabeth stared, alarmed. For the first time in days she took a good, long look at her twin. Despite the mornings spent out on the sunny ocean surfing, Jessica looked thin and pale. "What's the matter?" asked Elizabeth, her voice full of concern. "If you tell me, maybe I can help."

"I can't tell you," Jessica repeated in a hoarse whisper. "For his sake, for my sake, for . . . for *all* our sakes. Please just promise." She fixed desperate eyes on her sister's face. "Promise you won't breathe a word to anyone."

A dozen more questions sprang to Elizabeth's lips, but she didn't ask them. Jessica was in terrible distress, and that was the bottom line. Elizabeth put her arms around Jessica's slender shoulders, giving her a protective hug. "Of course I promise," she said. "Your secret's safe with me."

Jessica pulled back, dashing the tears from her face. "Thanks a million, Liz." She started toward the door. Then she turned and brushed Elizabeth's cheek with a quick, grateful kiss before disappearing into the hallway.

Elizabeth gazed after her sister, her forehead

furrowed with worry. Again, she'd gotten the distinct impression that Jessica was afraid of something—deathly afraid.

Jessica's secret was safe. Elizabeth would be true to her word. But was *Jessica* safe?

The newspaper-office light clicked off and the outer door slammed. From the corridor came the sound of a key turning in the lock. Ten seconds passed, and then, inside the office, the door to the *Oracle*'s large walk-in storage closet swung slowly open.

Ken stepped into the dim, deserted room, a copy of the Palisades High School *Pentagon* dangling from his hand. The color had drained from his tanned, handsome face, and his jaw was still trembling with shock at what he'd overheard.

Elizabeth and Jessica were gone, but their conversation seemed to reverberate in the air around him. Again, Ken heard Elizabeth's voice. *"You went to the beach and met that guy. How long have you been seeing him? Is it serious?"*

And Jessica hadn't denied it. She hadn't said, "What guy? What are you talking about? I go out with Ken. *He's* the boy I love." Instead, she'd cried—he'd heard the tears in her voice. Cried, and begged her sister to keep her secret.

Ken looked down at his hands. His fingers had

tightened on the Palisades High newspaper, and without thinking, he'd torn it in half and then in half again. Now he continued to shred the paper, a flush of rage and pain flooding his face as the reality of the situation sank in.

It explains all her crazy behavior lately, Ken thought grimly. *She's cheating on me!*

Chapter 9

In the locker room after football practice on Thursday, Ken spent a few extra minutes standing under the hot shower. He wished the water streaming down his face and body could cleanse him inside as well as out. *I don't want to feel anything,* he thought, his eyes tightly shut. *I don't want to know anything.*

With a sigh, he turned off the faucet. Then he wrapped a towel around his waist and walked back to his locker, his flip-flops slapping in the puddles on the cement floor.

Out of the corner of his eye, he checked out his teammates, who were busily getting dressed at their own lockers. Was it his imagination, or were some of them looking at him with pity and disdain? Had word got out that Jessica was seeing someone else on the sly? Was this one of those "the boyfriend's always the last to know" scenarios? *It could even be one of them,* he realized. *One of my teammates, my classmates.* But Elizabeth had questioned Jessica—she didn't seem to know him. So maybe he wasn't from Sweet Valley. A college guy?

Ken clenched his jaw. *It was bad enough, what went on with that Zack Marsden guy,* he thought, remembering the fling Jessica had had when she'd visited her brother at SVU recently. When Ken had found out about Zack, Jessica had promised never to stray again. And now here she was, apparently meeting some guy right out in the open, at the beach! *Is the whole school talking about it behind my back?*

Todd's locker was in the same row as Ken's. Having just wrapped up an intramural basketball game, Todd was sitting on the bench, pulling off his high-tops and socks.

"Hey, Wilkins," said Ken cautiously.

"What's up, buddy?"

Todd sounded breezy and unconcerned, not like someone keeping a major secret. But if anyone knew what was going on, Ken figured, it'd be him. *Liz probably tells him everything. They have that kind of close relationship.* The sour taste of betrayal filled Ken's throat. *The same kind I thought I had with Jessica.*

"Not much." Ken dialed the combination on his gym locker and pulled out a pair of clean boxers. "The usual. Guess I'll catch up with Jess, see if she wants to do something. Go to the beach or the mall or something."

"Hmm," mumbled Todd, stripping off his sweaty T-shirt.

"So." Ken put on his boxers and jeans and sat down. "The girls are acting kind of weird these days, huh?"

Todd grimaced. "Liz is driving me nuts. It's like she blames me for everything—I'm single-handedly responsible for the whole war with Palisades. And I can talk until I'm blue in the face, but I'll never get her to admit that we're justified in taking action against those guys."

"Jessica's been acting strange ever since last Friday night," said Ken. "She's the opposite of Liz, though. I mean, she's keeping quiet for the most part."

"There's a switch," said Todd with a laugh.

Ken mustered a smile. "Yeah. Well, I don't have a clue what's on her mind. I suppose she talks to Liz."

Todd shrugged. "Maybe. But at least she's not writing holier-than-thou editorials and campaigning for the Nobel Peace Prize. Enough is enough, you know? That's why I decided to have a party tomorrow night. It's time to have some fun. Everybody's too darned serious these days."

Ken relaxed somewhat, his spine slumping. Todd was pretty nonchalant. He didn't seem to be hiding anything, so maybe Elizabeth hadn't told him. Ken felt a little better believing that, but a little better than absolutely rotten still wasn't great. The basic fact hadn't changed. Jessica was cheating.

Ken had a sudden, violent urge to smash his fist into the hard, unyielding metal of the lockers. "When are we gonna get our act together and go bash some skulls in Palisades?" he burst out.

Todd cocked one eyebrow. "I thought you were only marginally into this stuff."

"No way." Ken raised his voice so the guys at the other lockers nearby could hear. All at once it seemed important that no one question his toughness. "I'm ready to nail those guys."

"Well, talk to Bruce about it. He's our drill sergeant."

Ken stuck his feet into his shoes. "I'll do that. Catch you later, Wilkins."

"Yeah, sure."

Ken strode out of the locker room, his chin jutting aggressively. He felt like picking a fight, but he also felt sort of like crying. *It's because I don't know what I'm dealing with,* he thought, wedging his tightly balled-up fists into the front pockets of his jeans. He hadn't got anywhere digging for dirt with Todd. He might as well go straight to the source. If he wanted to know what was going on, there was only one person to ask. Jessica.

When cheerleading practice was over, Jessica hurried to the parking lot, pulling a sweatshirt over her head as she went. The football players had also finished practice and were in the locker room showering. *Ken expects me to wait,* she thought, *but I just can't deal with him right now.*

She had her hand on the Jeep's door handle when a voice called out behind her. "Where are you rushing off to?"

Darn, I almost made it, Jessica thought. She spun around, a false smile on her face. "Oh, hi," she chirped brightly. "I was just—I thought I'd . . . I'm starving." She patted her stomach. "We had a killer practice. I need to refuel, you know? So I was going to dash home and—"

"Let's go to the Dairi Burger." Ken stood directly in front of her. His blond hair was still slick from the shower, and when he smiled, his teeth gleamed white and even. "My treat."

"Well . . ." There was no escape, no excuse she could make. Ken was her boyfriend; this was the kind of thing they always did together. "Sure. Sounds great."

Jessica cast one last longing look at the Jeep over her shoulder, then followed Ken to his Toyota. Strapping herself into the passenger seat, she flipped down the visor and got busy brushing her hair and checking her makeup in the mirror. She didn't want to have to look at Ken. *He'll see it written all over my face,* she thought, applying watermelon pink lip gloss. *He'll guess that I've been with someone else this very same day, that these lips have kissed another boy.*

"So you went surfing this morning," Ken remarked conversationally.

"Yeah." Jessica reached toward the dashboard and cranked the volume on the radio. *Change the subject, Wakefield,* she advised herself. *Fast.* "I just love this new Jamie Peters song, don't you?" she shouted over the blaring music. She started singing along.

Ken turned the car into the Dairi Burger lot. As they walked into the restaurant, Jessica spotted Amy and her boyfriend, Barry Rork, and nearly sobbed with relief. "Let's go sit with those guys," she suggested, waving.

Ken clasped her hand, stopping her. "I'd rather have a little time alone with you," he said. "Is that all right?"

"Sure, but—"

"Because I've been neglecting you." Ken squeezed her hand tightly. "You've been spending far too much time by yourself lately."

That's what you think! Jessica thought, almost laughing out loud in her nervousness. Helplessly, she let Ken lead her to a relatively quiet booth in the back. "Burger and fries?" he asked.

Jessica calculated the time it would take to eat a burger and fries. "You know, I'm not that hungry, after all. How about just getting a couple of shakes to go?"

Already on his way to the counter, Ken must not have heard the last part of her suggestion. He returned with two fresh strawberry milk shakes, a cheeseburger, and a large order of fries, and he showed no intention of leaving. "This is nice, isn't it?" he said, sipping his shake.

Jessica fiddled nervously with the paper wrapper from her straw. "Yeah."

"Back to your surfing." Ken looked her straight in the eye. "Are you taking lessons?"

Jessica thought about the informal instruction she'd received from Christian—surfing lessons and love lessons—and her face flushed beet-red. She pretended to choke on a mouthful of milk shake. "Um, uh." She coughed. "No. I, uh, I called Steve at college and asked him for a few tips. You know, since I'm using his board. And I just watch other people. It was easy enough to pick up the basics that way."

"Great. But how come you didn't tell me about it? Why keep it a secret?"

"Oh, well, I—I wanted to surprise you. I was going to tell you to watch Rock TV the day I entered the surf competition and you'd see me win and find out about it that way."

"When's the competition?" Ken asked.

Jessica couldn't remember. For all she knew, it had already come and gone. "Um, a week or two. I-I'm not sure."

Ken shook his head, smiling playfully. "Maybe I should be jealous of your hanging out with some cool surfing crowd."

"Oh, I don't hang out with them." She laughed, hoping she sounded relaxed and natural. "I'm a total lone wolf."

"Really?" Ken cocked his head. "That's not usually your style."

"It's just that I'm so . . . focused. On becoming a better surfer." Jessica slurped her milk shake, trying to finish it as quickly as she could so she could escape this torturous inquisition. "I'm not in it to meet people."

"Can I come with you sometime?"

This time Jessica really did choke. She coughed for a minute, holding a paper napkin over her mouth. "Must've gone down the wrong pipe," she said finally, smiling weakly. "Come *with* me? Sure, but I get up early. I mean, *really* early. It's still dark out, and it's really cold on the beach, but . . ." Ken watched her calmly. Jessica heard herself babbling. *Slow down,* she told herself. *Don't try so hard. Keep it simple.* "Sure you can come sometime. That would be fun."

Ken pushed away his empty glass. "In the meantime, how about tomorrow night?"

"What about tomorrow night?"

"Todd's having a party, but maybe we could do something before." He nudged her foot with his under the table. "Go for a drive and have a picnic someplace romantic, like Las Palmas Canyon."

"Tomorrow night."

"Yeah. You don't have other plans, do you?"

Her date with Christian wasn't until Saturday night. *I can't do it,* Jessica thought. *But I have to do it. I'm still Ken's girlfriend.* "No, of course I don't have other plans. A picnic. Todd's party. It'll be . . ." *Torture,* she thought dismally. ". . . fun."

She'd never been so happy to leave the Dairi Burger. Outside half an hour later, she took a deep, bracing breath of fresh air. *I made it,* she thought as Ken drove her home. *I'm still in the clear.* But she didn't feel good about what she'd just pulled off. One of these days Ken was bound to ask her an innocent question she couldn't answer. How many lies would she have to tell before it was all over?

* * *

Elizabeth and Enid reclined by the pool in the Wakefields' backyard Friday afternoon experimenting with the new suntanning lotion Enid had bought at the mall. "Supposedly it's a total sunblock," said Enid, squeezing a blob of lotion into her palm and then smoothing it over her bare legs, "but it also has some kind of magic bronzing agent so we'll get a deep, dark tan without skin cancer."

Elizabeth adjusted her sunglasses. "As long as it doesn't stink us all up and dye us terrible colors like that Tofu-Glo stuff Jessica used to sell door to door!"

The two girls were still giggling when the telephone rang. Elizabeth twisted in her chaise lounge to reach the portable phone. "Hello?"

"Is this Liz? It's Caitlin."

"Hi, Caitlin! How are you?"

"Not v-very good." Caitlin's voice trembled. There was a pause; she blew her nose discreetly. "It's Friday and I'm just so . . . so . . ."

Elizabeth had a hunch Caitlin had been crying and was now fighting back another bout of tears. "The weekends are the hardest," she commiserated gently. "I know you must really miss Doug."

"We always spent Friday night together. We had this routine, you know? We'd go to an old movie at the Plaza and then get Chinese food and then take a walk on the beach, and I just can't believe we'll never do those things again."

Elizabeth's heart ached in sympathy. "You have to try not to think about it. Go out and do something fun to distract yourself."

"There's no place in Palisades I can go without being reminded of Doug, though." Caitlin sniffled. "And I really don't want to run the risk of bumping into him and his new squeeze."

"Tell you what," Elizabeth said impulsively. "Come over here tonight. Todd's having a party."

Caitlin hesitated. "I don't know, Liz."

Elizabeth noticed Enid waving at her. "Hold on a sec, Caitlin." She covered the mouthpiece with her hand. "What?" she asked Enid.

"I don't know if that's a good idea, inviting Caitlin to Todd's party," Enid whispered. "Maybe you should ask Todd first."

"You mean because he made such a big deal about its being a closed party and keeping it secret?" Elizabeth snorted. "He's just being paranoid. Palisades isn't going to storm over here and trash his house."

"You never know, Liz," said Enid. "If Bruce and Todd and the rest of the gang found out some Palisades High guy was throwing a party, they'd jump at the chance to make trouble."

Elizabeth shook her head. "Caitlin hardly poses

a threat." She got back on the phone. "You've got to come over," she urged Caitlin. "I promise you'll have a great time."

"Are you sure I'll be welcome?"

For a split second it occurred to Elizabeth that Enid might be right—this might be a serious mistake. But she pushed the thought from her mind. "Of course you'll be welcome," she said. "Bring Marla, too!"

The party at 1010 Country Club Drive was in full swing when Elizabeth, Enid, Caitlin, and Marla pulled up. As they climbed out of Elizabeth's Jeep, Elizabeth put her head close to Enid's. "See? There are tons of people here," she hissed. "No one'll even notice Caitlin and Marla. Anyhow, everybody knows the war is with the Palisades guys, not the girls."

The four walked up to the pillared entrance of the Wilkinses' stately brick mansion, Elizabeth leading the way. Inside, they followed the sound of voices and music down the hallway to the spacious family room at the back of the house.

The room was packed full of teenagers, and the sliding glass doors were wide-open so the party could spill out onto the patio. Elizabeth, Enid, and the two Palisades girls entered just as the CD on the stereo ended. There was a pause before the next CD began, and suddenly Elizabeth realized that the music wasn't the only thing that had stopped. So had the conversation. In fact, complete silence blanketed the room, and everybody had turned to stare in their direction.

Elizabeth stepped forward, refusing to be intimidated. "Hi, Olivia," she said, waving to Olivia and her boyfriend, Rod Sullivan. "Hi, Rod."

Olivia smiled back wanly. Rod's expression remained blank. "Hi, Liz," said Olivia. "Uh, hi, Caitlin and Marla."

Another song kicked in and voices began to buzz again, but no one stepped forward to greet the newcomers. People moved away, turning their backs, so that Elizabeth, Enid, Marla, and Caitlin were left standing alone in a circle of empty space.

"Maybe this wasn't such a good idea," Marla murmured, nervously fiddling with the silver bangles on her left wrist. "Why don't we just leave? We could go out for ice cream, catch a movie."

"No," said Elizabeth stubbornly. "We're going to stay at the party and we're going to have fun!"

"It won't be much fun if no one talks to us," Caitlin whispered.

"They'll talk to us." Elizabeth grasped Caitlin's arm. "Come on."

She started to march Caitlin toward the snack

table, where Jessica, Ken, and some other kids were clustered. Before they'd taken two steps, however, someone blocked their path.

Elizabeth looked up into her boyfriend's unsmiling face. "Hi, Todd."

Todd didn't greet her with a kiss, as he usually did. "What's the story, Liz?"

Todd's face was tight with suppressed fury, but Elizabeth pretended not to notice. "What do you mean?" she asked, her tone light.

He gestured at Marla and Caitlin. "This is a closed party."

"Yeah, but they're here with me—they're my friends," said Elizabeth. "I thought it would be OK."

"Well, you thought wrong," Todd said bluntly. "Nobody from Palisades High is welcome in my house."

Elizabeth's cheeks flamed. She shot a mortified glance at Caitlin and Marla, who looked as if they wished they could sink into the floor and disappear. "Todd, can we go someplace else and talk about this?" Elizabeth asked in a low voice.

Todd folded his arms across his chest. "We can talk right here," he declared. "I don't mind their hearing what I have to say. They can take the message back to Palisades."

"What message?" Elizabeth exclaimed. "They're not spies."

"How do I know that?" Todd insisted.

Elizabeth couldn't believe Todd was being so paranoid. And she also couldn't believe that no one else was coming forward to tell Todd he was being ridiculous. *They're all just standing there staring,* she thought, *like we're some kind of carnival side-show.*

"Liz, if you lend us your keys, we can drive the Jeep back to your house and get our car," Marla said softly. "Then you can stay at the party and find a ride home with somebody later. I really think it would be best."

"No," said Elizabeth, her voice trembling with anger. She hadn't taken her eyes off Todd's face. Now he shifted his gaze away, and she felt vindicated—it proved he knew in his heart he was wrong. "If my friends aren't welcome here, then neither am I. Come on, you guys. Let's get out of here."

She did a sharp about-face and sailed out of the party, Enid, Marla, and Caitlin scurrying in her wake. She hoped Todd would call after her, but he didn't.

Her chin was still held high, but as soon as they were back outside in the driveway, Elizabeth's knees started shaking. She climbed behind the wheel of the Jeep and sat for a long minute before starting the engine. "I'm really, really sorry," she said to Marla and Caitlin. "I can't believe that just happened. If I'd had any idea Todd would—" She glanced at Enid, who just smiled sadly. Elizabeth sent her a silent message. *Thanks for not saying "I told you so."*

"It's OK," Marla said somewhat stiffly. "The same thing would probably happen if we took you to a party in Palisades."

Elizabeth revved up the Jeep and sped down Country Club Drive, eager to put Todd's house far behind them. "Let me make it up to you," she begged the girls. "How about banana splits at Izzy's Ice Cream Shop?"

In the rearview mirror she saw Caitlin and Marla exchange glances. "I don't think so," Caitlin said at last. "It sounds nice, but let's just call it a night."

They drove the rest of the way to Calico Drive in awkward silence. By the time she reached her house, Elizabeth was near tears. "This was sort of a rotten experience, but we can't let it push us apart," she said to Marla and Caitlin as the four of them stood in the driveway, preparing to say good-bye.

"I know," agreed Caitlin. "I lost Doug—I'd hate to lose you, too. But if anything, it's just going to get harder. People's feelings are more negative than ever."

"Promise you won't give up," Elizabeth pressed.

Caitlin nodded, but the smile she gave

Elizabeth was unconvincing. "Sure. We'll see you at the next task-force meeting."

The two Palisades High School girls drove off. Elizabeth and Enid stood in the driveway, watching them go. When the car was out of sight, Elizabeth turned toward the house with a heavy sigh. "Caitlin's right," she said to Enid, wiping a tear from her cheek. "It's just going to get harder. Maybe there's no future for our friendship."

"It's not fair!" exclaimed Enid. "Why should we have to sacrifice our friends to prove our loyalty to our school?"

Elizabeth shook her head. "I don't know. And I don't know if it's worth it, either. Sweet Valley High isn't the same old school we've always known and loved. It's changing because of this war with Palisades." She stared pensively into the darkness, wishing she could read the future, but it was as murky and blank as the starless night sky. "Changing," she repeated. "Maybe forever . . . and not for the better."

Chapter 10

The telephone rang at nine the next morning. Elizabeth put down the spoon she was using to scoop the seeds out of a cantaloupe and reached for the phone on the kitchen wall. "Hello?"

"Liz, it's me," Todd said.

"Oh." Elizabeth's whole body tensed. She tossed a scoopful of seeds into the sink and turned on the garbage disposal for a few seconds. "Hi."

Todd cleared his throat. "Um, about last night."

Elizabeth remained pointedly silent. She wasn't about to give him any help.

Todd started again. "What happened at my party. I'm really, uh . . ." She could tell he was almost choking on the word, but finally he got it out. "I'm sorry."

Elizabeth slumped against the kitchen counter,

immeasurably relieved. Part of her had feared she'd never hear from Todd again. "I'm sorry, too," she said quietly. "I should've asked you first, like Enid said. The whole night was a huge mistake."

"If you'd just given me some warning," Todd agreed, also sounding relieved. "You caught me off guard is all."

"That's your excuse?" Elizabeth's anger flared again. "We caught you off guard and your first instinct was to be outrageously rude? Great, I feel much better."

"Look, I said I was sorry," Todd snapped. "I felt terrible after you left, and I didn't sleep a wink last night worrying about whether you'd ever talk to me again. What more do you want from me?"

Elizabeth twisted the phone cord around her finger, frowning. *That's just the problem,* she thought. *I don't know what I want from you. Maybe I want you to say sorry like you* mean *it.* "Let's just put it behind us," she suggested.

"Sure. So what about tonight? Are we still on?"

They always went out on Saturday night—it was a given. *Like Friday night used to be a "given" for Caitlin and Doug. . . .* "Of course," Elizabeth replied.

"We'll do something special," said Todd. "I'll make up to you for last night, Liz. I swear. Give me one more chance, OK?"

"One more chance," Elizabeth agreed.

Suddenly, though, her hand trembled as she replaced the telephone receiver. She and Todd both had spoken lightly, but Elizabeth feared there was a darker truth lurking behind the casual phrase. One more chance. She couldn't help wondering if that meant this was their *last* chance to make things right again.

"You have to study?" Ken asked. "On a Saturday night?"

It was the first excuse that had popped into Jessica's mind. She regretted the lie immediately, but it was too late to backtrack and change her story. She really did have a biology test on Monday—that much was true. "Yeah." Jessica switched the phone from her right ear to her left and giggled nervously. "I'm so far behind in Russo's science class, you know? Ordinarily I'd just cram the night before, but I can't leave it till the last minute this time because I practically have to read the whole textbook."

"Maybe we can do something tomorrow, then," said Ken. "You'll need a study break at some point."

"Yeah," Jessica agreed, careful not to make any promises. "Well, have a nice night."

"You, too."

"Right. With my books!"

"With your books," Ken echoed. "See you later."

"Bye."

Jessica hung up the phone before Ken could initiate the "I love you," "I love you, too" routine and danced across her bedroom in her underwear, humming. Yanking open her closet door, she rifled through her dresses and skirts. "Something short, something sexy," she murmured, eyeing a red miniskirt. She pushed the skirt aside, fingering a gauzy green dress. It was long but sheer, and on a breezy night by the water . . . "It'll cling to my legs and drive Christian absolutely wild," she decided, tossing the dress onto her bed.

As she considered sandals and jewelry, though, she started laughing at herself. Granted, it had been a couple of days since they'd seen each other, but would Christian really go wild over a sexy dress? So far they'd spent all their time together on the beach, in bathing suits or skintight wet suits—for all purposes, practically naked. Christian had seen her legs—every inch of them.

But tonight is going to be special, Jessica thought, shimmying into the tank top. She slipped on a pair of dangly silver-and-turquoise earrings and tossed her hair, admiring the effect in the mirror. *Our first real nighttime date.* They had planned to meet at their usual beach parking lot and then drive to a cozy little out-of-the-way restaurant up the coast. It was bound to be a million times more romantic than making out in the back of the VW bus. She and Christian would be experiencing each other in a whole new way, and she wanted him to fall more madly in love with her than ever.

Jessica ransacked the top drawer of her dresser for a bottle of Rendezvous perfume she'd borrowed from Elizabeth and had conveniently forgotten to return. As she dabbed perfume behind her ears, at the base of her throat, and on her wrists, she could feel her pulse racing. She was excited at the prospect of meeting Christian, but also anxious. She tried not to think about the fact that she'd told Ken she had to study, but it kept popping into her head. Guilt mixed with her delirious anticipation.

Guilt . . . and a tiny measure of fear. She and Christian were leaving the safe haven of their early-morning surfing lessons, the privacy of their secluded beach. They were going out in public.

It was a risk, but one Jessica was willing to take. She remembered the previous night, going with Ken to Todd's party: the dishonesty, the secret misery of playacting the role of Ken's devoted girlfriend. Tonight she planned to seize happiness with both hands. She wouldn't have to fake it with Christian.

Winston stuck a hand into the bowl of microwave popcorn. "This is the life," he said, grinning up at Maria. They were lolling on the couch in his family room and his head was pillowed on her lap. "Popcorn with real butter—none of that 'lite,' less-filling stuff. On the tube, an action flick—no dialogue, just lots of car chases. And the most adorable girlfriend in the history of the human race."

Maria laughed. "You are one lucky guy."

"I am." Winston's expression grew serious. "And, you know, this is what I'm *supposed* to be doing with my free time. Hanging out with you, not roaming back alleys with Bruce pretending to be some Clint Eastwood 'make my day' type."

Maria bent her head so that her dark hair fell in a curtain around them. Her full red lips were just an inch from his own. "How about making *my* day?" she whispered provocatively.

Winston closed his eyes blissfully. It felt like years since he'd skulked around the Palisades High School parking lot in search of a white Toyota Corolla. For the first time in ages, he was perfectly relaxed . . . and primed to be thrilled from head to toe by a long-overdue romantic interlude with Maria.

But just as their mouths met in a kiss, the telephone rang. "I'm not picking it up," Winston mumbled.

It rang twice, three times, four times. Maria squirmed. "Isn't the answering machine on?" she asked.

"Guess not," said Winston, pulling her close again.

"I can't stand it," she declared after eight rings. "If you don't get it, I will!"

With a groan Winston twisted, stretching to reach the phone on the end table. "Hello," he said, his tone grouchy.

"Winston, it's Todd."

"Hey, buddy." Winston sat up. "What's happening?"

"We got word that Palisades is about to pull some kind of stunt in Sweet Valley," muttered Todd. His voice was low and clipped—he spoke fast, as if he were worried about being overheard. "We're meeting at the warehouse, OK? In fifteen minutes."

"Fifteen minutes? Well . . ." Winston hesitated. It was so nice to curl up with Maria and forget about the high school war. But if his pals needed him . . . "Yeah, all right." Winston rolled his eyes at Maria, who stuck out her lower lip in a disappointed pout. "I'll be there."

"Good," said Todd.

Before Winston could pump his friend for more details of the supposed Palisades plot, he heard a click and then a dial tone. Winston hung up the receiver, his forehead wrinkled. "We're having some kind of emergency meeting, about Palisades. But Wilkins sounded weird," he commented. "Not like himself."

"All you guys are weird these days," complained

Maria, swatting Winston's arm with a throw pillow. "You're obsessed. It's boring. Not to mention dangerous and really, really dumb." Now it was her turn to frown. "You're not off to slash more tires, are you? Because one of these days, if you don't cool it, you're going to get into big trouble."

Winston stuck his feet into his sport sandals and tightened the Velcro straps. "I can't blow them off," he said. "Whatever's going down, I need to be there. If nothing else, I can try to keep the guys in line, keep them calm and reasonable."

"Yeah, right," Maria said sarcastically. "You've been this successful so far."

Winston clenched his jaw. "I'll just keep trying. Anyhow, it's not like I have a choice. If I don't show, the guys'll never speak to me again."

Maria sighed. "Just . . . be careful."

Winston laughed. "Most of the time all we do is talk. The biggest danger is getting spit on by Bruce when he starts making speeches and foaming at the mouth."

They kissed again, and then Winston walked Maria out to her car. As she drove off, he lifted his hand in a good-bye wave, then slid behind the wheel of his old orange VW bug. Meeting his friends at the abandoned warehouse was the last thing he felt like doing, but he'd told Maria the truth: He didn't have a choice. Unless he wanted to be completely friendless, he had to back up his buddies. But while he was willing to be a soldier in the war against Palisades High, ever ready to march into battle, he was going to keep on looking for a way to steer the guys in the direction of peace.

"Jess, have you seen my perfume?" Elizabeth called through the bathroom. She stepped into her sister's room. "The new stuff. Rendezvous."

Jessica handed the bottle to Elizabeth. "Hot date?"

"Yeah, sort of. I mean, no, it's just the usual. Out to dinner someplace, maybe a movie, maybe a drive."

"So why the perfume and the short skirt?" wondered Jessica, turning away from her sister to fluff her hair in the mirror.

Elizabeth smoothed her hands down the skirt of her short knit dress. It *was* a little sexier than she usually dressed for a run-of-the-mill date with Todd. "We decided that we need to take time out and focus on each other, talk about something other than what's happening at school. Find some common ground again—remember why we fell in love with each other in the first place. Things are pretty rocky."

"What's the problem?" asked Jessica, carefully outlining her mouth with a lip pencil.

"We've been fighting nonstop about the war

with Palisades High." Elizabeth uncapped the bottle of perfume and sniffed it. "Don't tell me you haven't noticed! You were at the party last night—you saw that scene."

Jessica shrugged. "I guess I've been preoccupied."

It was the opening Elizabeth had been waiting for. "You look like you're going out, too," she observed. "With Ken?"

Jessica didn't answer, but her cheeks flushed scarlet.

"Jess," said Elizabeth.

"What?" Jessica's tone was defensive.

"I know you said that you can't tell me anything about this mysterious surfer guy, but—"

"So don't make me say it again, Liz," begged Jessica.

"Don't you trust me?"

"Of course I trust you," Jessica said. "But I still can't tell you about him. Someday you'll understand, but for now *you* have to trust *me*."

Jessica's hand trembled, making it hard for her to apply her mascara. A chill ran up Elizabeth's spine as she watched her sister. The twins shared a special psychic bond, and Elizabeth could sense what Jessica was feeling at that moment. Excitement, guilt, and something else.

Fear again.

The intuition hit Elizabeth with the force of a freight train. *Something out there—or someone—may harm her.* "Be careful," she whispered.

Jessica met Elizabeth's eyes. "I'll be OK, Liz," she promised, but her voice shook slightly.

There was nothing else Elizabeth could do or say. As she returned to her own room, though, her arms were still sprinkled with goose bumps.

It should have been just another Saturday night in Sweet Valley, California. Just another date for Jessica, for Elizabeth and Todd. But nothing was ordinary anymore. *Anything could happen tonight,* Elizabeth thought with a shiver. *Anything at all.*

Ken sat slumped in the driver's seat of his car. He'd parked half a block from the Wakefields' house on Calico Drive, midway between two streetlights so he'd be in shadow. For almost an hour he'd watched Jessica's driveway, waiting for her to drive off or for some guy to drive up. Twenty minutes earlier, Todd had picked up Elizabeth, but otherwise there'd been no action.

A shred of hope quivered in Ken's heart. *Maybe she wasn't lying,* he thought. *Maybe she* is *staying in to study tonight.* But what about the conversation he'd overheard in the *Oracle* office? What about her strange behavior, going to the beach every morning before school? Jessica had pretty much confessed to Elizabeth that she met someone there, but when Ken asked her about it, she swore she was always on her own. *Something's going on,* he admitted to himself with a heavy sigh. At this point it was just a question of how bad that something was.

Maybe I don't want to know the gory details. Ken put a hand on the key in the ignition. He could head home, and then if Jessica went out, he wouldn't know anything about it. He'd just hang back and wait for her to come clean with him. "Wait for her to break up with me, rather," he muttered. Pain shot through him, and his chest and throat tightened with tears he refused to let flow. No, he couldn't turn his back on this. He had too much self-respect. *And I love Jessica,* he thought. *I've invested a lot in our relationship. If I'm going to fight for her, I have to know what—who—I'm fighting against.*

He continued to slouch in the dark car. The sun had long since set and the night was cool. He'd forgotten to bring a sweatshirt, so he hugged himself against the chill. Then he saw something that made him sit up, the blood rushing hot to his face.

Jessica, wearing a long, flowing skirt, emerged from the side door of her family's house. As Ken squinted, trying hard to see in the dusk, she climbed behind the wheel of the Jeep and turned on the engine and headlights. As she backed the Jeep out of the driveway, Ken started the engine of his own car.

This is it, he realized. He gave Jessica a head start, waiting until she reached the stop sign at the end of the block. Then he eased the Toyota away from the curb and followed her at a conservative distance, his jaw clenched with tense determination. No matter how much it might end up hurting him—and hurting Jessica—he was going to get to the bottom of this.

Chapter 11

Ken kept his foot lightly on the accelerator, maintaining a steady speed. He let a couple of cars move in between him and the Jeep—he could still see Jessica, but he was pretty sure she hadn't noticed him. In the dark he'd be just another pair of headlights in her rearview mirror.

He still couldn't quite believe this was happening. *I'm spying on my girlfriend, tailing her like some cut-rate private eye in a bad movie,* he thought. Where would she lead him? What would he see?

Reaching the coast highway, Jessica stepped on the gas. *She's sure in a hurry,* Ken noted, his anger returning. *The other day at the Dairi Burger and last night at Todd's party, she couldn't get away from me fast enough, and now she's risking a speed-*

ing ticket to be with someone else! It made him so mad, red spots danced in front of his eyes. He hammered his fist upward, punching the roof of his car. "Cool it, man," he counseled himself. "You don't know for sure what's going on." After all he and Jessica had shared together, he owed it to her to give her the benefit of the doubt. She was innocent until proven guilty. *Please don't be guilty,* Ken found himself praying silently. *Please let this be a huge mix-up.*

Ahead of him, Ken saw Jessica's brake lights flash suddenly. She slowed down, then switched on her left turn signal and swung into the small beach parking lot where Ken and Elizabeth had found her the other day. Just short of the entrance to the lot, Ken pulled over on the sandy shoulder of the road and turned off his headlights. He could see the Jeep from there without being detected.

Just like the other day, there was only one other vehicle in the lot. It was hard to tell in the dark, but it looked like a light-colored van. Ken's eyebrows furrowed. The same one that was parked there before?

He rolled down his window so he could see better. For a moment the Jeep was dark; Jessica had killed the engine. Then the interior light went on briefly as she opened her door and climbed out.

There was no motion or signal of any kind from

the van, but in a few steps, her skirt billowing in the night breeze, Jessica was at the passenger-side door. Before she even touched the handle, the door swung open. She hopped in. An instant later the van's engine rumbled to life. The driver stepped on the gas, and the van shot across the parking lot, roaring onto the highway in a cloud of dust.

For a few seconds Ken just stared after the departing vehicle. It had all happened so quickly, he hadn't had time to react, to leap out and confront Jessica and her mysterious date. *She did meet somebody,* Ken thought, his stomach lurching. And was that or was it not the same powder blue van from the other day? *It must be. She was with him then, too.*

Ken pulled back onto the highway, stepping hard on the gas pedal. He felt miserable and betrayed, but he also felt determined. He might not like where this road seemed to be leading, but he'd committed himself. He had to follow it to the end—he had to learn the whole truth.

Jessica twisted in her seat and studied Christian's somber profile. "You seem distracted." She placed a tentative hand on his knee and laughed nervously. "I thought you'd be happier to see me."

"I *am* happy to see you. Are you kidding? And

you look great." Christian glanced at her, his eyes smoldering with love and admiration. "I feel as if I never noticed how beautiful you are."

It was just what Jessica wanted to hear. "So focus on me," she urged playfully. "Forget the rest."

Christian stared straight ahead at the highway, which curved and rolled as it followed the rugged coastline. "I wish I could," he said, "but the world isn't going to go away just because we want it to."

Jessica sank back in her seat with a sigh. "What happened today?"

"I did what I said I'd do. I talked to the guys." Christian's fingers tightened on the steering wheel. "Man, talk about a bad scene. At first they thought I was joking when I said we should declare a truce with Sweet Valley. Then, when they realized I was serious and they could count me out of any stunts they might be planning to pull in the future . . ."

He stopped, as if it were too painful to continue.

"I'm sorry," Jessica said softly. "Maybe they're wrong, but they're still your friends."

"They *were* my friends. Past tense," Christian corrected her bitterly. "It was during lunch, you know? A kind of strategy meeting. Well, after I made my big speech, they basically kicked me out of the room. They weren't going to talk while I was there—said they thought I might turn them in. I told them I wasn't a Benedict Arnold, but that didn't make a difference. 'Either you're one of us, or you're one of them'—that's how McMullen put it."

Jessica slid her hand up Christian's arm to lightly massage the back of his neck. "You did what you thought was best," she said. "And, hey, look at it this way. You gave them something to think about. Maybe they'll come around to your point of view."

"I doubt it." As she rubbed his shoulders, Jessica could feel the tension radiating through Christian's entire body. "I don't know any details because, like I said, they kicked me out. And for the rest of the day nobody talked to me—I got the cold shoulder from every single one. But something's up tonight."

"I'm so tired of this stupid war ruling my life," Jessica declared impatiently. "Let's not worry about it anymore, OK? I mean, so what if Palisades High plays another prank on Sweet Valley High—how bad could it be? They'll probably just egg the Sweet Valley guys' houses again, or slash their tires."

"No." Christian shook his head. "That's not how it works. Haven't you noticed? The whole thing about violence is that it *escalates*. It goes from bad to worse. We've seen bad. Now get ready to see worse."

Christian's tone was ominous and Jessica shivered despite herself. As they drove up the coast, they were leaving Sweet Valley and Palisades far behind. *But what's going to happen while we're gone?* she wondered. *What will we come home to?*

"I still think we should try to forget about it," she told him, her eyes beseeching. "We have a chance to escape it for a few hours. Let's not waste our time together."

"I'll try, Jess. You know I'm crazy about you—I've been looking forward to this evening more than anything. But I can't promise I'll be the best company."

"Tell you what." Jessica leaned close so Christian could feel her body pressing against his arm and smell her perfume. "I can't do it now because we'd crash the van, but when we get to the restaurant, I'll give you a kiss one hundred percent guaranteed to chase all other thoughts out of your brain. What do you say? Will you give me a chance?"

Christian grinned. "You bet. And if the first kiss doesn't work, I'll let you try a second time. And a third time, and a fourth."

The mood felt suddenly lighter, and Jessica relaxed. They drove a few more miles, listening to the new Jamie Peters tape, which Christian had popped into the cassette deck. But when a lively rock tune gave way to a mournful ballad, Jessica's mood seesawed again in response.

She stared ahead at the dark ribbon of road. Christian was driving at the speed limit, but suddenly Jessica felt as if she were in some kind of spaceship, traveling at lightspeed away from the known world. *We don't know what's happening back there,* she thought, *and we don't know what's ahead of us, either.* They'd taken some drastic steps: Christian had cut himself off from his friends, and she was getting closer and closer to breaking up with Ken. The wheels were in motion; it was too late to stop. When she'd climbed into Christian's VW van tonight, she'd taken an irrevocable step. The question was: Was this the end or the beginning? Or both?

Winston braked at the stop sign at the intersection of Fenno Avenue and Cedar Street on the outskirts of Sweet Valley. When he let out the clutch to move forward, the orange VW bug stalled. "I need a tune-up," Winston muttered to himself, turning the key in the ignition and stepping on the gas. After a few coughs and rattles, the engine *putt-putted* to life. "Heck, I need a whole new car!"

He got the bug going again and continued on Cedar Street, leaving behind a modest residential neighborhood and entering an area zoned for industry. There were a few businesses still in operation—an auto mechanic, a discount furniture store—but most of the buildings had SPACE TO LEASE signs out front. *There's the street that leads to the renovated warehouse where the dance was held,* Winston noted as he passed Phantom Lane. If he remembered correctly, it was about half a mile to the abandoned warehouse where Bruce had led the Sweet Valley High gang after the fight.

His car stalled again at the next stop sign. "Should've hitched a ride with Wilkins," Winston chided himself. Now that he thought about it, he was kind of surprised Todd hadn't offered to give him a lift. *Guess he had other things on his mind,* Winston decided. *Like this meeting tonight.* Todd had sounded really strange, not like himself at all. *Obviously he knows something I don't.* Winston was suddenly apprehensive. What was on the agenda? He hoped it didn't involve another trip to Palisades and more vandalism. *Because I don't think we'd get away with it a second time. Those guys would be waiting for us. . . .*

Winston steered the VW bug down a side street. If he wasn't mistaken, that long, low building up ahead was the warehouse. "Where is everybody?" he wondered out loud. He didn't see any other cars parked nearby—the block was deserted. "I guess I'm the first one."

He slowed down, considering the possibilities. He *could* keep circling the block until someone else showed up. *But Patman would give me hell for being a wimp,* he told himself, *and it's not like I'm afraid to walk in there.*

He parked the car in an alley adjacent to the warehouse, taking his time about setting the parking brake, rolling up all the windows, and checking that the doors were locked. At the last minute he unlocked the car again to rummage around under the seats. "Shoot, I forgot to bring a flashlight," he grumbled. "How am I going to be able to see what I'm doing?"

He stuck his hands in the front pockets of his khakis and peered at the shadowy warehouse, which was scrawled here and there with graffiti. In the feeble glow of a far-off streetlight, the broken windows looked like staring eyes. *Maybe I should wait here for one of the other guys,* Winston thought. *I could break my neck trying to climb in a window without a flashlight.* Then he considered how it would look if he was skulking around in the parking lot when Bruce and the rest of the group arrived. He had to prove himself.

Taking a deep breath, Winston walked toward the warehouse. He really didn't want to be doing this—his skin was crawling—but he managed a pretty good imitation of a macho swagger. *Just get here fast, guys,* he pleaded silently.

He was about to heave himself up onto a broad windowsill when he noticed a small door at the corner of the building. It was slightly ajar. As a gust of wind swept past, the door groaned open a few inches wider. "Why do things the hard way?" Winston asked himself, brushing the dirt off his hands. "This isn't Hollywood and I'm not a stuntman."

When he reached the door, however, he hesitated for a split second. It was pitch-black inside, and tentacles of cold, clammy air oozed out, wrapping around him. *Just do it,* Winston said to himself. *The worst that can happen, there'll be bats.*

He strode boldly into the cavernous warehouse, whistling through his teeth. Ahead of him, he thought he heard a noise, like a shoe scuffling on concrete. "Hello?" he called, squinting hard to see in the blackness. "That you, Wilkins?"

No one answered. Winston took another step forward. Again there was a scraping sound, but this time, before he could speak, someone grabbed him around the shoulders, immobilizing him. When he started to shout for help, a hand clapped roughly over his mouth.

Winston had no idea who had tackled him or what was going to happen next, but he knew one thing. He was in big, big trouble.

Chapter 12

Elizabeth sat in the passenger seat of Todd's black BMW, staring straight ahead. They were parked at Miller's Point, a turnout in the hills overlooking Sweet Valley. Below them, the lights of town twinkled warmly. Farther off, the moon cast a path of silver on the ocean.

Sweet Valley used to be the most picture-perfect place on earth, thought Elizabeth. But lately, with her own classmates—her own boyfriend!—getting involved with violence and vandalism . . . *maybe it's not paradise anymore. Maybe we're not even safe at home.*

Todd had turned off the engine, and they'd both unbuckled their belts, but although they'd come to Miller's Point dozens of times before to talk and kiss, tonight neither seemed to know what to do next. An unaccustomed silence stretched between them, growing more and more uncomfortable as the minutes passed.

Finally Elizabeth shot a glance at Todd's stony profile. She cleared her throat and spoke. "I feel like I'm parking with a stranger," she confessed quietly.

"This isn't working," Todd agreed. "I thought we could come here and work up an appetite before dinner, just pretend everything was the same as always, but somehow . . ."

The sentence trailed off, unfinished. "It's like there's this huge wide space between us even though we're only a foot apart," Elizabeth said softly. "This *distance*." She fought back panic and fear, but reality stared her in the face. *This could be the last time Todd and I ever park at Miller's Point.* "How did it happen so fast?"

"It's this damned high school war," said Todd. "It's turned everything upside down."

Elizabeth thought about Caitlin and Doug, breaking up after two whole years together, and her eyes filled with tears. "I don't want to feel this way," she choked out. "I don't want to sit right next to you and feel like I can't reach over and touch you. But I'm so *mad*! It's all your fault, you know. You decided this stupid war is more important to you than I am."

"I did not!" Todd protested. "You're the one who's too stubborn to try to see things from my point of view. It's been black and white for you from the beginning. Once you made up your mind I was one of the bad guys, I didn't stand a chance."

"I *did* try to see things your way," Elizabeth exclaimed, indignant. "But it's pointless trying to have a rational conversation with someone who's in total testosterone overdrive!"

"Well, if you weren't such a hysterical female," countered Todd, "maybe you'd—"

"Hysterical female?" Elizabeth cut in, her eyes flashing. "*Hysterical* female?"

She was perilously close to slapping Todd across the face. *That's what happens in the movies in scenes like this,* she thought somewhat irrelevantly.

Before she could say or do anything else, though, Todd's hands were on her shoulders. He pulled her toward him so abruptly, she cried out. "Hey, what do you think you're—" Then his mouth was on hers and she was silenced by a fierce, passionate kiss.

A moment later Elizabeth drew back breathlessly. *He really deserves a smack now,* she thought. *So how come I feel like kissing him again?* She mustered up an outraged manner. "What's the big idea?"

To her surprise Todd grinned, his eyes crinkling at the corners. "Must be—how'd you put it?—testosterone overdrive."

Suddenly they both burst out laughing. Elizabeth collapsed against Todd and he folded his arms around her. "Darnit!" she declared ruefully. "Maybe that's what's made me mad more than anything. I still love you, no matter how dumb you and the guys have been acting lately."

"If you ever stopped loving me, I don't know what I'd do." Putting a hand gently under her chin, Todd tilted her face so she was looking up at him. "I guess that's why I'm starting to see that you were right. We *did* go too far the other night, slashing those tires. I know better. But I let the macho thing sweep me along."

"I can't relate to any of it," she said, "but you know what I think? It's OK to disagree. Arguing like we were just now is better than not having anything to say to each other. But we need to be able to respect each other. There are some things I couldn't live with, like more vandalism and fighting."

"And I won't ask you to live with that," Todd vowed. "I need you to be proud of me, Liz, not ashamed of me. And I need to respect myself, too. I thought we could get respect by standing up to Palisades, but there was nothing manly or brave about sneaking over there and slashing those guys' tires behind their backs."

All at once Elizabeth's heart felt immeasurably lighter. "We're going to get past this, aren't we?

We're not going to break up like Caitlin and Doug!"

Todd hugged her close again. "No way. You're stuck with me, Wakefield. Maybe I don't always agree with your editorials, but I'm nuts about you."

"I'm nuts about you, too," she whispered, her lips seeking his for another kiss.

They continued to kiss blissfully for ten solid minutes. Then Elizabeth surfaced for air. "We were going to go out for dinner," she reminded Todd.

He smiled down at her. "Who needs food?"

They kissed again; then Todd grew serious. "Thanks, Liz," he murmured, burying his face in her silky blond hair.

"For what?"

"For not going easy on me. For having faith in me. For having faith in *us*."

"I'm just glad we both realized what was really important before it was too late," Elizabeth said.

"You matter to me more than anything, and I promise I won't lose sight of that again," said Todd. "I promise from now on I won't let GNOs and the rivalry with Palisades distract me from my most important job, which is making *you* happy."

Elizabeth was still concerned about Jessica, but as she smiled up at her boyfriend, her other big worry dissolved like mist in the morning sun. *I was crazy to think this could destroy me and Todd,* she thought.

Their skirmish had ended peacefully. Maybe it was a good omen—maybe it was the start of a general trend. Maybe the high school war was almost over!

Greg McMullen hammered his fist into Winston's gut. Winston doubled over, coughing and gasping. He wrenched his right arm as hard as he could, but the struggle was futile. He couldn't fight back, because his arms were tightly pinned behind his back by another Palisades guy, a heavyweight wrestler, by the feel of it.

Please let me be dreaming, Winston thought dizzily. *This can't really be happening. I didn't walk into the warehouse and get ambushed by a posse from Palisades.*

But he heard and felt his shoulder blades crack as the guy's grip on him tightened. All too clearly, he could see by the flickering light of a couple of camping lanterns the cruel faces of the boys gathered in a circle around him. And the pain in his stomach where he'd been punched half a dozen times already—he wasn't dreaming that.

It hadn't been Todd who'd phoned him earlier. His Sweet Valley buddies wouldn't be joining him at the warehouse. Winston had walked straight into a trap. It was a setup.

"So, Egbert," sneered McMullen. "What kind of

idiot name is that anyway? Egbert." The other Palisades guys chortled. "You made a big mistake the other night when you slashed the tires on Jake Watson's car."

A tall boy with a blond crew cut stepped forward from the circle. "My dear Watson, I presume," quipped Winston in a Sherlock Holmes–style English accent.

Jake Watson was wearing a ripped black T-shirt with a skull and crossbones on the front. He didn't laugh at Winston's little joke. When Jake spoke, Winston recognized the voice he'd heard the other night as he'd narrowly made his escape from the Palisades High parking lot. "You're dead, man," Jake Watson had asserted then.

"I could just make you fork over the dough it cost to fix my car," snarled Jake, "but that would be too easy. All you Sweet Valley kids are stinking rich—what's a few bucks to you? Naw." He shook his head. "I decided it's better to make an example of you."

An example of what? thought Winston. *Dead meat, maybe.* He really didn't want to stick around to find out. But how was he going to get out of the warehouse in one piece when he was surrounded by a whole football team's worth of angry—not to mention enormous—Palisades High guys?

"Hey, you know what?" said Winston cheerfully. "I'm starting to get the feeling this is a case of mistaken identity. You think I slashed your tires? Do I really look like the kind of person who'd do something like that?"

He tipped his head comically to one side, making his goofiest face. Jake Watson didn't crack a smile. "Yeah, you look like the kind of person," said Jake. "I saw you with my own eyes."

"Might not have been me," Winston insisted. "Might have been my twin brother, Rocky Egbert. Now you wouldn't want to mess with Rocky, so you shouldn't mess with me, either, or ol' Rock'll have something to say about it."

He was just kidding around, trying to lighten the mood. *Heck, we're just a bunch of teenagers,* Winston thought. *We think our school's better than theirs, they think theirs is better than ours. Maybe we went a little overboard, should've stuck to waving pom-poms at football games, but we don't have to act like we're engaged in World War III.*

No one laughed at his joke, though. Winston tried again. "So did you hear the one about the two Palisades High students who walk into a juice bar and this guy from Sweet Valley says—"

"Shut up," Jake snapped.

"Yeah, you don't get it, do you, Egbert?" Greg McMullen stepped forward again. Involuntarily, Winston flinched, anticipating another punch. McMullen grinned. "That's right. There's more where that came from. But first we want to talk to you, and we don't want any of your cruddy humor."

"I could talk a lot better if the gorilla who's holding me would let go," Winston said amiably. "And how about a change of venue? Someplace a little more sociable, a booth at the Dairi Burger, perhaps. How's this for a deal—the shakes and fries are on me."

Again, no one smiled or laughed. "You don't know when to stop yapping, do you, Egbert?" said Greg McMullen. He raked his eyes around the circle of malevolent faces. "OK, somebody show this guy that actions speak louder than words."

One of the bullies stepped forward, a muscle-bound kid with shoulders about six feet across. Before Winston could say a word in his own defense, the boy's fist had slammed into his ribs.

Winston's knees buckled. He gulped down the sob that rose in his throat, making a massive effort to hold himself together. No matter what they did to him, no matter how bad the pain, he wouldn't give in to the urge to cry—he wouldn't give them the satisfaction. They could hurt him, but they couldn't humiliate him.

Winston gritted his teeth. "C'mon, guys," he said, managing to keep his voice from shaking. "You've made your point, now let me out of here."

"You think we're through with you? He thinks we're through." Jake Watson glanced at the rest of the gang, and they laughed. "We're not through with you, Egbert. We haven't even *started* making our point."

Time to call their bluff, Winston decided. "OK, fellas. You know you won't get away with this. I've got a good look at all of you. If you let me go now, I won't turn you in to the cops."

"Actually, we're not worried about your being able to identify us," said Jake, "because when we *are* through with you . . ."

As he stepped forward, Jake lifted one hand. By the flickering light of the lanterns, Winston saw a glint of silver. His eyes widened with terror. Was it a knife . . . or a gun?

Either way, it didn't look good. Winston raked the shadowy warehouse with desperate eyes, searching for a way out. *But there isn't one, unless these guys let me walk*, he realized, his heart sinking into his sneakers. For the first time it occurred to him that the boys from Palisades High might do more than punch and scare him. Maybe he was about to become the first real fatality of the high school war. Maybe they were going to *kill* him.

Christian pulled the VW minibus into the sand-swept parking lot of the Beachcomber Cafe, a tiny restaurant perched high on a bluff overlooking the

Pacific. Hand in hand, he and Jessica walked toward the entrance to the restaurant. "Isn't this the greatest escape?" said Jessica. "I really feel as if we've got away from it all. Away from Sweet Valley, from Palisades, from the rivalry. Away from our usual old selves. We can be who we really want to be here."

"It's like magic," Christian agreed. He draped his arm around her shoulders. "And you know who I want to be?"

She looked up at him, her smile radiant. "Who?"

"Just a regular guy, madly in love with the sexiest, most beautiful girl in the world."

They stepped through the door into the foyer of the cafe. Jessica peeked past the unoccupied hostess stand. "Isn't this fun? I think we're the only ones here," she told Christian.

"In that case . . ." He clasped her waist in his hands, turning her to face him. "How about that kiss you promised me? The one that's going to make me forget everything else?"

"Are you sure you can handle it?" she teased.

"Try me."

"OK." She looked around to make sure no one was watching, then lifted her face to his, her lips parted invitingly. "Prepare for meltdown."

Christian bent his head, and she twined her arms around his neck. When their lips met, an electric current shot through her body from head to toe. "Wow," whispered Jessica. "Let's do that again."

The second kiss was even more passionate than the first. Jessica felt herself being transported. *As long as this kiss lasts, we really* are *the only two people in the world,* she thought.

She was swept away by the delirious pleasure of the moment, but not so completely that she didn't notice a movement out of the corner of her eye. Someone had entered the foyer. *The host, or a waiter,* Jessica thought distractedly, too happy to be embarrassed. *Oh, well. Nothing this good could last forever.*

With a delicious, regretful sigh, she opened her eyes a little wider, looking past Christian's shoulder. Then she focused on the figure standing in the doorway, and her heart stopped beating.

A rangy, broad-shouldered blond guy in khakis and a blue polo shirt stood just inside the entrance to the cafe, an expression of mingled shock, hurt, and anger contorting his handsome face.

Jessica's heart started up again, but now it was hammering with guilt and horror. She tore herself from Christian's embrace. "Ken!" she cried.

Chapter 13

Elizabeth and Todd walked into the Dairi Burger holding hands. For some reason, tonight their usual hangout with its worn vinyl booths, Formica counter, and vintage jukebox seemed more romantic than an elegant candlelit restaurant. "How come this feels like a first date?" whispered Elizabeth.

Todd squeezed her hand. "Because we're starting fresh. Getting to know each other all over again."

Elizabeth wanted to cuddle in one of the booths at the back, but as soon as they entered, they were hailed by friends at a couple of different tables. Todd was leading her toward some of his basketball buddies, when Elizabeth noticed Maria beckoning. "Let's just say hi," Elizabeth suggested.

They reversed directions, weaving through the

noisy, crowded restaurant. Maria was sitting in a booth with Lila and Amy.

"Have a seat," said Amy, gesturing to the jumbo order of fries in the middle of the table. "There's plenty to go around."

Elizabeth and Todd squeezed into the booth. Maria leaned forward, elbows on the table. "What are *you* doing here?" she asked Todd.

Todd raised his eyebrows at the question. "Well, you may not have noticed, but"—he winked at Elizabeth—"I'm going out with this really fabulous girl. And I wanted to impress her, so I brought her here. Nothing but the best, right? I'm going all out, no expense spared, so go ahead, Liz. Order whatever you want on the whole menu. Get a burger. Get a *cheese*burger! You can even have your very own plate of fries. That's the kind of guy I am—a real high roller."

Elizabeth giggled, but Maria still looked puzzled. "No, what I mean is, I thought you were with Winston," Maria said. "At the emergency GNO."

Now it was Todd's turn to wrinkle his forehead. "What emergency GNO?"

"The meeting. Weren't you the one who called him a little while ago?"

Todd shook his head. "I didn't call him."

Maria frowned. "I could've sworn . . . well, somebody called him and said there was going to be a meeting. You know, to talk strategy about Palisades and all that. We were watching a movie, but when Winston heard that, he raced off like it was really important. But if it was so important, why aren't you there?"

"I've been out with Liz, so if anybody tried to call me, I wouldn't have been home," explained Todd. "But I didn't think anything was scheduled for tonight. Hold on a minute. Let me just check something."

Todd slid out of the booth. The girls watched him stride across the restaurant to the pay phone by the back door. "This is weird," said Maria, distractedly munching a french fry. "Why would Winston know about this meeting when Todd doesn't?"

Elizabeth reached for a fry. "Like he said, we were out for . . . a drive." She blushed slightly, remembering how much fun she and Todd had had kissing and making up at Miller's Point. "So if Bruce or whoever called the meeting at the last minute . . ."

Before they could speculate further, Todd returned to the table, his expression dark with worry. "I just talked to Patman," he announced. "He didn't call Winston and he can't think who else might have. There is no strategy meeting tonight."

"But somebody called Winston, and he took off like a shot and—" Suddenly Maria's face went pale. She clapped a hand over her mouth. "Oh, no," she whispered.

The same horrible possibility had occurred to all of them simultaneously. Elizabeth turned to Todd, her eyes wide and anxious. "Todd, do you think the Palisades High guys might have tracked Winston down somehow?"

"They must have called him up and pretended to be one of his friends, and he walked right into their trap," Maria wailed.

"It's starting to look that way," said Todd grimly. He jumped to his feet. "C'mon. We've got to find him before—"

Todd bit off the sentence without completing it. Elizabeth met Maria's eyes and saw her own fear magnified a hundredfold. She guessed they were all thinking the same thing. Was Winston facing the vengeance of Palisades High all by himself? Would his friends get to him before it was too late?

The horrible moment seemed to last an eternity. Jessica was paralyzed, her feet cemented to the floor of the Beachcomber Cafe foyer, her uplifted arm frozen in a gesture of supplication. Only her eyes moved, darting desperately from Ken to Christian and back again. *Oh, no,* she thought desperately. *What have I got myself into?*

"Ken, I—I can explain," Jessica stammered.

Ken took a step forward, his expression harsh

and unforgiving. "OK, Jess," he snapped sarcastically. "Let's hear it."

"I . . . we . . ." She faltered. *What can I say? "It's not how it looks?" It is how it looks. It's worse than how it looks.* Ken had caught her in the arms of another man. She'd never in her life looked or felt or been more guilty. *Please let me just sink through the floor and disappear.*

Jessica seized desperately on the fact of Ken's presence at the Beachcomber Cafe. Surely it wasn't a coincidence. "What about *you*?" She placed her hands on her hips, indignant. "I can't believe you actually followed me!"

"Why not?" countered Ken, his face flaming. "You've been lying to me. I should've gone on blindly trusting you? And the whole time . . ." He choked to a stop, then spit out the words with an effort. "You." He was glaring at Christian now, and with a sinking heart, Jessica realized that Ken recognized the other boy. "The fight. You're from Palisades."

Christian stood with one hand resting protectively on Jessica's shoulder. He didn't respond to Ken's baiting tone. "I think we should go," he said quietly to Jessica.

Jessica couldn't have agreed more. But exiting the restaurant was going to be a problem with Ken blocking the door.

And apparently Ken wasn't ready to leave. He stared at Jessica and Christian. "It's bad enough that you're running around on me," he said, hoarse with rage and anguish, "but running around with somebody from Palisades High? How could you?"

Suddenly, for the first time, Jessica fully comprehended what was happening. After weeks of hiding and lying, Ken had discovered her secret. In an instant her relationship with him had been shattered forever. "Ken, I never meant to—"

"You didn't just betray me, Jessica." Ken's voice shook. "You're betraying your friends, your school, your town."

Jessica's eyes brimmed with tears. "No. It's not like that."

"Yes, it is." Ken's mouth twisted with disgust. "How can you show your face in Sweet Valley when you're doing this?"

"Ken, please. Can't we just—let's go somewhere and talk."

"I don't have anything to say to you." Ken stabbed a finger in Christian's direction. "You I'll see again, and I'll make you pay for this. But you . . ." His eyes raked Jessica from head to toe. She felt naked and horribly, horribly guilty. "I never want to see you again."

With that, Ken turned around and stalked out of the cafe.

* * *

Elizabeth, Todd, Maria, Amy, and Lila huddled by the pay phone at the Dairi Burger. "Do you know where Winston was going?" Todd asked Maria, his deep voice vibrating with urgency.

Maria bit her lip. "I just assumed the meeting was at Bruce's house. That's where you guys always seem to hang out for GNOs. I'm pretty sure he didn't—" She shook her head. "No, he didn't say where he was headed. But the conversation was pretty short. Wherever it was, it didn't need a whole lot of explanation."

Todd stuck a coin in the phone and dialed rapidly. "Patman?" he said. "Maria's not sure where Winston was going, but it sounds like whoever called him didn't say much and Winston didn't ask many questions. So my guess is the abandoned warehouse."

Todd listened to Bruce for a moment. Elizabeth held her breath. *The abandoned warehouse,* she thought. *Where the guys hid out the night of the fight!*

"Right," Todd said after a moment. "We should go over there together, since we don't know what we'll find. I'll wait for you. But make it quick."

He slammed down the phone and then picked it right back up again. He punched in a number. "Matthews isn't home," he muttered, drumming his fingers on the wall. "I know—I'll try his car phone."

Todd dialed again, but Ken didn't pick up his car phone, either. "I'll try again in a couple minutes," Todd said. After making a few other brief calls, he hurried outside with Elizabeth and the others on his heels.

Bruce was just pulling into the Dairi Burger lot, the Porsche's tires squealing. Within minutes a dozen other boys had also arrived.

Todd jogged over to Bruce's car. "Wait!" Elizabeth called after them. "What should *we* do?"

He glanced back at her. "Wait here," he advised. "We'll be back soon. And don't worry," he added, with a tight smile for Maria. "Winston'll be all right."

Elizabeth, Maria, Lila, and Amy stared after the departing cars. Elizabeth turned to Maria and saw tears spilling down the other girl's cheeks. Elizabeth slipped an arm around Maria's waist and echoed Todd's assurance. "Don't worry, he'll be all right."

"Maybe, but I can't just sit around here chewing my fingernails," Maria declared, dashing the tears away. "I have to do something."

Elizabeth felt exactly the same way. "Let's go to the warehouse," she said.

Maria was ready to jump right into her car, but Amy hesitated. "Do you think it's safe?" she asked. "I mean, if the Palisades High guys are at the warehouse doing . . . doing something to Winston, and our guys show up, there's going to be a fight that makes the scuffle the other night at the dance look like a shuffleboard match."

Amy's words got Elizabeth thinking, and a jumble of terrifying possibilities crowded her brain. "You're right," she said. "The Palisades guys are bound to be really mad about the tire slashing. They could be planning to do the same sort of thing. What if they have knives? What if they're *armed*?"

The color drained from Maria's face. "We've got to do something."

"Call the police," said Lila.

Elizabeth nodded. It worked the night of the dance—a major rumble had been averted. "The guys won't like us interfering," she predicted, "especially if it turns out to be a false alarm, but they'll thank us later."

Just then Enid drove up in her mother's small blue hatchback. She pulled up next to the girls and rolled down her window. "What's going on?" she asked.

"Oh, Enid!" Elizabeth exclaimed. "I'm so glad you're here. But I don't have time to explain—I have to go call nine-one-one!"

With those words Elizabeth dashed back into the Dairi Burger, leaving Enid openmouthed behind her.

* * *

Once again Jessica and Christian were alone in the foyer of the Beachcomber Cafe. But nothing was the same—it wouldn't be ever again. In just a few minutes Jessica's whole world had changed, irrevocably, forever.

"I'm sorry about that scene," Christian said, brushing her tear-streaked cheek with gentle fingertips. "I'm sorry it had to end that way between you two."

Jessica nodded numbly. She'd been thinking about breaking up with Ken for weeks, ever since she'd fallen for Christian. And even though she'd tried to be discreet, she always knew when she sneaked off to be with Christian that they ran the risk of someone's seeing them together and spreading the word to her boyfriend. But now that it had happened, she was suddenly overcome with sorrow and regret. "I did this all wrong," she sobbed. "He's always treated me so well—I shouldn't have two-timed him, I should've been more honest. It's not fair that he had to find out like this."

Christian rubbed her shoulder. "Don't be too tough on yourself. It's hard to see a situation clearly when you're right in the middle of it. And maybe you weren't really sure what you wanted before, and that's why you put off making the break with Ken. Making the choice."

Jessica looked up at Christian, her eyes wide.

He's right, she thought. *I wasn't ready before. But now I have to choose, ready or not, and if I choose Christian . . .*

Ken had spelled out in no uncertain terms what that choice represented. *"Running around with someone from Palisades—you're not just betraying me, Jessica. You're betraying your friends, your school, your town. How can you show your face in Sweet Valley?"*

If she chose Christian, Jessica realized, she'd be crossing over to the other side. Ken's wounded pride would transform itself into a fierce desire for vengeance against Palisades, and the rest of the guys were sure to back him up one hundred percent. When word got out, the high school war would rage hotter than ever.

I'm cutting myself off from my friends, thought Jessica. *I'm declaring myself an enemy of Sweet Valley. It won't just be Ken who hates me—no one will speak to me.*

As she gazed into Christian's caring eyes, love surged in Jessica's heart. He was worth it, worth everything she had to sacrifice and suffer. Hadn't he been willing to cut himself off from *his* friends in order to try to bring peace between the two schools, to create a safe, quiet space for their love to bloom?

Peace. The concept jolted Jessica back to reality. "I have to talk to Ken," she declared. "A lot's hanging in the balance, and right now he has the power to make things worse with just one word. But maybe if I talk to him and apologize and help him understand . . ." Jessica wasn't exactly sure what she was afraid of, but she knew the danger was out there, looming larger all the time. It was like a bomb she had to defuse. "Maybe I can keep something terrible from happening."

"Whatever you think's best," agreed Christian. "Tomorrow, when he's had a chance to cool off a little—"

"No." Jessica grabbed Christian's arm and pulled him toward the door. "It has to be tonight. It has to be *now*. In case Ken's rushing off to do something . . . rash." She remembered they'd driven in Christian's VW bus—she couldn't just hop into the Jeep and take off. She lifted imploring eyes to Christian. "I've got to follow him. We've got to follow him. Will you help me?"

Christian hesitated, but only for an instant. Then he nodded. "Let's go," he said briskly, "before he gets too much of a head start."

Time stood still for Winston as if the world had stopped turning on its axis. *How long have I been in here?* he wondered, his brain foggy with pain. How long had he been a prisoner in the musty, dank warehouse, surrounded by leering, cruel faces illuminated only by guttering lanterns? And how much longer could he take the beating?

His face was slick with blood from a cut on his forehead. If there were tears mixed in, he didn't know it. He was so numb now, he didn't feel like crying anyway, and he didn't have the strength to protest. In a strange, disembodied way, he felt resigned to his situation. *They're just making an example of me,* he thought. *They'll pulverize me, but they won't kill me.*

A second later somebody's fist hammered his face. Blood oozed out of Winston's nose, dripping down onto his shirt. *At least I hope they won't kill me,* Winston thought. *Please don't kill me, guys.*

He didn't realize he'd spoken the words out loud: "Please don't kill me." But his tormentors laughed. "You're not worth killing," Greg McMullen scoffed. "We just want to give you something to remember us by. We want to make sure the message comes across loud and clear: If Sweet Valley High messes with Palisades High again, every guy in the whole damned school is going to look like you look right now."

Another punch was aimed at Winston's middle, and he closed his eyes, steeling himself to endure the blow. Instead of the sound of a fist on flesh, however, he heard a loud tinkling smash. The Palisades boys shouted in surprise as broken glass showered down on them. "Hey, what the—Someone threw a brick through the window!" Jake Watson bellowed.

A moment later the door crashed open and a blinding light sliced into the darkness. Winston blinked in astonishment as a dozen or more figures burst into the warehouse. When the Palisades guy who'd been restraining him released Winston's arms, Winston nearly collapsed in relief. "Todd!" he croaked. "Bruce!" His friends had come to his rescue!

With a roar Todd and the other Sweet Valley boys charged forward in unison, Bruce holding his superpowered flashlight high. Greg, Jake, and the rest of the Palisades gang turned away from Winston to meet them. Instantly Winston realized the downside of the situation. In order to save him, his friends had been forced to walk right into the lions' den. *It's going to be the fight to end all fights,* he thought groggily.

The Sweet Valley group had taken Greg McMullen's crew by surprise. But the advantage was short-lived. In the all-out brawl that ensued, it was quickly apparent that the two sides were perfectly matched.

Winston dodged among the flailing bodies, looking for a way to help his friends best their opponents. Todd wrestled with Jake Watson while Bruce boxed with Greg McMullen. Before Winston could land any punches of his own, the door burst open again. *Reinforcements,* Winston guessed. This could turn the tide. But for which side?

Then he saw that the newcomers were girls. And not just any girls. Maria, Elizabeth, Enid, Lila, Amy!

A brick flew through the air—probably the same brick that had broken the window. The warehouse echoed with grunts and curses. "What are you doing here?" Winston bellowed, stumbling over to the girls.

Wide-eyed with terror, the five took one look at Winston's bruised face and bloodstained shirt and began to scream hysterically.

Winston wanted to shield them from the violence. But as he reached Maria's side, he felt his knees buckle. After the beating he'd just suffered, he was in no condition to protect anybody from anything. And all around them, the fight was growing more and more vicious. *My buddies saved me,* Winston thought, *but who's going to save them?*

Chapter 14

Elizabeth didn't think she was the type to faint at the sight of blood, but one look at Winston's blood-caked face and red-splotched shirt, and she had to clutch Enid's arm to keep from collapsing.

"What did they do to you?" Maria shrieked, her eyes wide with horror.

"I'm all right," Winston assured her, but his speech was slurred by a fat lip and he couldn't walk straight. "You guys better get out of here, though. Now."

He put an unsteady arm around Maria and tried to propel her toward the door. Elizabeth, meanwhile, ignored his advice and ran in the other direction. "We've got to stop this fight!" she called to Enid, Amy, and Lila.

But after a few steps she stopped, paralyzed by

confusion and fear. The fight was the most frenzied and violent she'd ever witnessed. *It's like a scene from a movie,* she thought, *only these aren't actors. They're not pulling punches, and that's not fake blood.*

It was dark and dusty in the warehouse, almost impossible to tell who was who. Amy and Lila were screaming at the boys to stop, but their pleas seemed only to add fuel to the fire. Elizabeth recalled what the girls had concluded that night at her house, when they'd learned that the guys had gone to Palisades High to slash tires and Elizabeth had wanted to chase after them and intervene. "If we show up and they feel like they have to protect us, it'll only make things worse," DeeDee had said.

It's true, Elizabeth thought as Todd caught sight of her and roared over his shoulder, "Get out of here!"

She didn't do as he ordered. She couldn't. She was rooted to the spot, both horrified and fascinated by the spectacle before her. She couldn't leave while Todd and her other friends were engaged in such a ferocious battle—she couldn't leave not knowing what might happen to them.

At that moment the person Todd was fighting—a husky boy with a blond crew cut—hurled Todd to the ground and then flung himself down on top of him. "Todd!" Elizabeth cried out at the sound of bone crunching on bone.

But if Todd was injured, he didn't show it. Bunching his muscles, he hurled the guy off him. Still grappling, they rolled over and over on the ground, oblivious to the fragments of broken glass lying everywhere.

Elizabeth wanted to close her eyes and blot out the nightmarish vision before her. She wanted to block her ears to the sounds. But the fight roared like a cyclone around her—she was trapped in the very heart of it. *They'll tear each other to pieces*, she thought, tears streaming down her face like rain. And what if someone had a weapon? One or more of the boys could end up with worse than cuts and bruises and broken bones. They could end up dead.

Elizabeth knew she'd made the right decision calling the police. But what if they didn't get to the warehouse in time?

Christian and Jessica drove down the dark coast highway in pensive silence, a heavy sense of foreboding weighing upon them. Jessica felt as if she were hurtling through outer space, toward some cold, black unknown. *What am I going to say to Ken?* she wondered, chewing her lip. *What will people at school think when they find out about Christian?*

For a couple of miles theirs was the only vehicle on the road. Then, ahead in the distance, a pair of taillights came into view. "That must be him," Jessica breathed, clasping her hands tightly together in her lap. She'd been half hoping Ken had got too great a head start, that they wouldn't catch up with him, but now it looked as if another confrontation was inevitable . . . and only minutes away.

Christian stepped on the gas. Slowly, the gap between the two cars closed, and Jessica was able to tell for certain that it was Ken's Toyota in front of them. "Where's he going?" she said out loud as Ken swerved abruptly off the highway, taking a turn a few miles short of the Sweet Valley exit. "There's nothing down that road but an abandoned railway station and a strip of crummy old warehouses."

"Remember the warehouse where the dance was held?" Christian said. "We're coming at it from a different direction, but it's down this way somewhere."

"Why would Ken be going there, though?"

"Maybe he's not going there." Christian shot a glance at Jessica. "You know, I'm thinking about how my Palisades friends were talking today. Something was in the works, you know? And that night, after the fight . . . we all took off, and me and my friends holed up at the deserted railroad station, and we found out later that the Sweet Valley guys did the same thing somewhere else."

It still didn't make sense to Jessica. "So you think Ken's heading for a hideout of some kind?"

"I don't know what I think." Christian's words were clipped and tense. "I just have a bad feeling about this neighborhood. Like I said, the Palisades guys were planning something, and whatever it turns out to be, it's not going to be good news for Ken and the rest of your friends."

They tailed the Toyota at a conservative distance as it turned left on a side street, then right, then left again. The area was gloomy and dark, with occasional streetlights broken or fizzling. Jessica stared out the car window at the boarded-up buildings and shuddered, remembering the last time she had traveled these forsaken streets. *The night of the dance*, she thought. *I drove here with Ken, but I left in a police car, with the sirens blaring.*

Sirens. Suddenly Jessica sat up straighter in her seat. "Do you hear something?" she asked Christian.

She rolled down her window and they both listened intently. Sure enough, the sound of distant sirens vibrated through the murky night air. "The cops," Christian said grimly. "I knew it. I knew there'd be some kind of trouble tonight."

"Maybe it's just a coincidence," Jessica said hopefully. "Maybe it's nothing to do with what Ken's up to, with anybody we know."

Christian didn't argue with her, but a minute later it became clear that his hunch had been right. The sirens were growing louder, and the sky pulsed with light. They cut through an alley, still following Ken's Toyota, and suddenly found themselves in the parking lot of a vacant warehouse just a hundred yards away from half a dozen Sweet Valley police cars and an ambulance, all with emergency lights flashing and sirens going full blast.

Ahead of them, Ken slammed on his brakes and parked haphazardly in the middle of the lot. As Ken jumped out of his car and raced toward the warehouse, Jessica stared at the chaotic scene, shocked by its eerie similarity to the scene of the last full-fledged fight between Sweet Valley High and Palisades. Her heart sank. Was history repeating itself?

When Elizabeth heard the sirens approaching, she nearly fainted with relief. "Thank goodness," Enid cried, gripping Elizabeth's arm. "I was starting to think they'd never get here, that maybe they thought it was a prank call."

"This is so terrible," Amy said, her voice quivering. "How could we ever have thought the fighting was glamorous and exciting, Li?"

Lila shook her head mutely, her face pale.

Enid pulled Elizabeth toward the door, but

Elizabeth hung back. She'd hoped the sound of the sirens would cause the guys to break it up, but if anything, the fighting became even more frenzied and brutal. She wanted to drag Todd away, but she was scared to get too close to the struggling bodies. "Todd!" Elizabeth called. "Please. Please, stop!"

The sirens were suddenly much louder. Elizabeth guessed that the police had just pulled up outside. All at once a few of the Palisades High guys made a break for the door while a couple others scrambled over the sill of a broken window at the back of the building. The boy Todd had been fighting headed for the door, but instead of letting him go, Todd chased him down and tackled him.

"They're insane!" Lila cried. "There are cops all over the place. Don't they know when to quit?"

The fight, still going strong, poured from the warehouse into the parking lot. Elizabeth and the other girls dashed outside on the boys' heels.

Elizabeth sucked in her breath when she saw what awaited them. Police cars formed a semicircle around the entrance to the warehouse, making escape impossible. A dozen officers ran forward, some blowing whistles, others wielding billy clubs.

Two policemen went straight for Todd, who was straddling his fallen opponent, pinning the boy's shoulders to the ground with his knees. *He'll let the guy go now,* Elizabeth thought. *The show's over. It's time to cool off.*

But Todd seemed unaware of the approaching policemen. He didn't appear to hear the sirens, the whistles, the commands to stand and put his hands in the air—he was too busy taking advantage of his opponent's complete immobility. Over and over, Todd raised his fist and with all his might punched the blond boy in the face. Blood spurted from the boy's nose, but Todd didn't let up.

Elizabeth stared at her boyfriend, stunned. Could this really be the same sweet, gentle, good-natured Todd who earlier in the evening had promised her he wouldn't have anything more to do with the high school war? Todd's eyes were like black holes in a face twisted with fury; his lips pulled back in a snarl as he panted from the exertion. *He looks more like an animal than a human being,* Elizabeth thought, fearing for Todd in a whole new way. *What's happened to him?*

Todd raised his fist one more time. Before he could land another punch, though, the two police officers seized his arms and hauled him to his feet. Still lying on the pavement, the Palisades boy rolled onto his side, curling his body into a ball and moaning.

"You're coming with us," one of the policemen informed Todd sternly. With a swift gesture, the officer wrenched Todd's arms backward and snapped on a pair of handcuffs. "Let's go. Into the car."

"Hey, Palisades started this fight," Todd protested. "They trapped our buddy and beat him to a pulp. We were just—"

"I said, get in the car," the officer barked. *"Now."*

The policeman propelled Todd toward a squad car. Elizabeth hurried after them. "Please, Officer," she called. "We just wanted you to break up the fight. Can't you just—"

Her voice was lost in the noise and confusion. As they marched toward the car, the officer read Todd his Miranda rights. "You have the right to remain silent, the right to obtain legal counsel, the right to—"

Elizabeth's jaw fell open in disbelief. She'd dialed 911 because she thought Todd needed police protection. Instead, he was under arrest!

Jessica shoved open the door and leaped out of the van. Christian climbed out, too, but after taking one step forward, he halted, his hands in his pockets. "No point going over there," he muttered, as if to himself. "I'm too late to help my buddies out, even if I wanted to."

Leaving Christian behind, Jessica walked forward slowly, riveted by the drama before her. Police swarmed over the parking lot, using billy clubs to pry the fighters apart. She spotted Bruce, Aaron,

Bill, Zack, in various states of struggle. A boy—from Palisades or Sweet Valley?—was helped onto a gurney and then lifted into the ambulance. Meanwhile, even from a distance, Jessica could tell that Winston was hurting. His face was a blood-streaked blur, and he leaned heavily on Maria's arm, as if he couldn't stand unaided. *What are Liz, Maria, and Lila doing here?* Jessica wondered. And were her eyes playing tricks, or was that Todd being dragged off in handcuffs?

She started to hurry over to her sister and then stopped abruptly. Someone was blocking her path. Ken turned and stared her straight in the face.

Her own mouth too dry for speech, Jessica waited in vain for Ken to say something to her. He didn't utter a word. Instead, for what felt like an eternity, he just looked at her, his lips set in a harsh, unforgiving line.

Jessica tried to muster up the nerve to defend herself. *Don't look at me that way,* she wanted to say. *I behaved badly and I hurt you, but I'm not evil!* But before she could speak, Ken turned away from her and strode over to the other Sweet Valley High boys, who were now standing in a huddle talking with a couple of police officers.

A gust of cool night air blew past Jessica, ruffling her hair and her gauzy skirt. She hugged herself, shivering. Ken was gone, but the icy anger she'd seen in his eyes seemed to remain, forming a wall between her and the rest of the scene, forcing her to keep her distance, to stay apart.

He's about to tell them, she thought with a feeling of doom. In a minute everyone would know all about her treachery. One by one, their faces would take on the same look of shock and anger and disgust that had twisted Ken's features into an unrecognizable mask. *Aaron, Bruce, Winston, Maria, Lila, Amy, Enid, Todd. Even Liz, my own sister. They'll hate me, disown me.*

She retreated a few steps, out of the circle of light and back into the shadows. She could never rejoin that group. No matter how she begged, they'd never again welcome her as one of them.

There was only one person she could count on to go on loving her.

Whirling, Jessica melted back into the night, returning to Christian's side.

"Liz, what's going on?" someone shouted. "What are they doing to Wilkins?"

Elizabeth spun around. Ken had just arrived on the scene, and now he grabbed her arm. "We've got to stop them," she told Ken, her eyes wild. "They're making a huge mistake."

As Ken's attention shifted to the injured Winston, Elizabeth ran after Todd and the policemen.

"Officer, wait!" she called. She was prepared to leap into the squad car—if she couldn't prevent them from arresting Todd, at least she could go with him for moral support.

"Thanks, Ms. Wakefield," said the policeman who'd handcuffed Todd, "but you've done your part. We'll handle it from here."

At the policeman's words, Todd froze. Then his head whipped around and he glared at Elizabeth, naked rage in his eyes. "*You* called the cops?" he barked.

Elizabeth flinched. "I-I was worried. We were *all* worried. Maria, Amy, Lila—we thought you guys might be walking into a trap and it would be safer for everybody if—"

"You don't understand what we're trying to do and you never will," Todd cut in. "So why didn't you mind your own damned business?"

The police officer shoved Todd toward the car. As Todd bent to climb in, Elizabeth clutched his sleeve. "Todd," she said desperately, her face wet with tears, "I'll follow you to the station. I'll post bond for you."

"Don't do me any favors," Todd said bitingly.

The car door slammed. Elizabeth staggered back as the policeman behind the wheel revved the engine and the car lurched forward, spitting gravel. In the backseat Todd stared straight ahead, not once glancing out the window in her direction.

There was mayhem all around as the other boys involved in the brawl were crowded into squad cars. And could that possibly be Jessica, standing in the shadows at the far end of the parking lot? Elizabeth couldn't focus on anything but the departing car. *It's taking Todd away,* she thought, her heart breaking. *It's taking him away from me forever.*

The rivalry between Sweet Valley High and Palisades High continues to escalate . . . with Jessica and Elizabeth caught in the middle. When the smoke clears, will the twins ever be forgiven? Find out in the final book of this fiery three-part miniseries, **A Kiss Before Dying.**

Bantam Books in the Sweet Valley High series
Ask your bookseller for the books you have missed

#1 DOUBLE LOVE
#2 SECRETS
#3 PLAYING WITH FIRE
#4 POWER PLAY
#5 ALL NIGHT LONG
#6 DANGEROUS LOVE
#7 DEAR SISTER
#8 HEARTBREAKER
#9 RACING HEARTS
#10 WRONG KIND OF GIRL
#11 TOO GOOD TO BE TRUE
#12 WHEN LOVE DIES
#13 KIDNAPPED!
#14 DECEPTIONS
#15 PROMISES
#16 RAGS TO RICHES
#17 LOVE LETTERS
#18 HEAD OVER HEELS
#19 SHOWDOWN
#20 CRASH LANDING!
#21 RUNAWAY
#22 TOO MUCH IN LOVE
#23 SAY GOODBYE
#24 MEMORIES
#25 NOWHERE TO RUN
#26 HOSTAGE
#27 LOVESTRUCK
#28 ALONE IN THE CROWD
#29 BITTER RIVALS
#30 JEALOUS LIES
#31 TAKING SIDES
#32 THE NEW JESSICA
#33 STARTING OVER
#34 FORBIDDEN LOVE
#35 OUT OF CONTROL
#36 LAST CHANCE
#37 RUMORS
#38 LEAVING HOME
#39 SECRET ADMIRER
#40 ON THE EDGE
#41 OUTCAST
#42 CAUGHT IN THE MIDDLE
#43 HARD CHOICES
#44 PRETENSES
#45 FAMILY SECRETS
#46 DECISIONS
#47 TROUBLEMAKER
#48 SLAM BOOK FEVER
#49 PLAYING FOR KEEPS
#50 OUT OF REACH
#51 AGAINST THE ODDS
#52 WHITE LIES
#53 SECOND CHANCE
#54 TWO-BOY WEEKEND
#55 PERFECT SHOT
#56 LOST AT SEA
#57 TEACHER CRUSH
#58 BROKENHEARTED
#59 IN LOVE AGAIN
#60 THAT FATAL NIGHT
#61 BOY TROUBLE
#62 WHO'S WHO?
#63 THE NEW ELIZABETH
#64 THE GHOST OF TRICIA MARTIN
#65 TROUBLE AT HOME
#66 WHO'S TO BLAME?
#67 THE PARENT PLOT
#68 THE LOVE BET
#69 FRIEND AGAINST FRIEND
#70 MS. QUARTERBACK
#71 STARRING JESSICA!
#72 ROCK STAR'S GIRL
#73 REGINA'S LEGACY
#74 THE PERFECT GIRL
#75 AMY'S TRUE LOVE
#76 MISS TEEN SWEET VALLEY
#77 CHEATING TO WIN
#78 THE DATING GAME
#79 THE LONG-LOST BROTHER
#80 THE GIRL THEY BOTH LOVED
#81 ROSA'S LIE
#82 KIDNAPPED BY THE CULT!
#83 STEVEN'S BRIDE

#84 THE STOLEN DIARY
#85 SOAP STAR
#86 JESSICA AGAINST BRUCE
#87 MY BEST FRIEND'S BOYFRIEND
#88 LOVE LETTERS FOR SALE
#89 ELIZABETH BETRAYED
#90 DON'T GO HOME WITH JOHN
#91 IN LOVE WITH A PRINCE
#92 SHE'S NOT WHAT SHE SEEMS
#93 STEPSISTERS
#94 ARE WE IN LOVE?
#95 THE MORNING AFTER
#96 THE ARREST
#97 THE VERDICT
#98 THE WEDDING
#99 BEWARE THE BABY-SITTER
#100 THE EVIL TWIN (MAGNA)
#101 THE BOYFRIEND WAR
#102 ALMOST MARRIED
#103 OPERATION LOVE MATCH
#104 LOVE AND DEATH IN LONDON
#105 A DATE WITH A WEREWOLF
#106 BEWARE THE WOLFMAN (SUPER THRILLER)
#107 JESSICA'S SECRET LOVE
#108 LEFT AT THE ALTAR
#109 DOUBLE-CROSSED
#110 DEATH THREAT
#111 A DEADLY CHRISTMAS (SUPER THRILLER)
#112 JESSICA QUITS THE SQUAD
#113 THE POM-POM WARS
#114 "V" FOR VICTORY
#115 THE TREASURE OF DEATH VALLEY
#116 NIGHTMARE IN DEATH VALLEY
#117 JESSICA THE GENIUS
#118 COLLEGE WEEKEND
#119 JESSICA'S OLDER GUY
#120 IN LOVE WITH THE ENEMY
#121 THE HIGH SCHOOL WAR

SUPER EDITIONS:
PERFECT SUMMER
SPECIAL CHRISTMAS
SPRING BREAK
MALIBU SUMMER
WINTER CARNIVAL
SPRING FEVER

SUPER THRILLERS:
DOUBLE JEOPARDY
ON THE RUN
NO PLACE TO HIDE
DEADLY SUMMER
MURDER ON THE LINE
BEWARE THE WOLFMAN
A DEADLY CHRISTMAS
MURDER IN PARADISE
A STRANGER IN THE HOUSE
A KILLER ON BOARD

SUPER STARS:
LILA'S STORY
BRUCE'S STORY
ENID'S STORY
OLIVIA'S STORY
TODD'S STORY

MAGNA EDITIONS:
THE WAKEFIELDS OF SWEET VALLEY
THE WAKEFIELD LEGACY: THE UNTOLD STORY
A NIGHT TO REMEMBER
THE EVIL TWIN
ELIZABETH'S SECRET DIARY
JESSICA'S SECRET DIARY
RETURN OF THE EVIL TWIN